New Fiction

A NEW DIRECTION

Edited by

Sarah Marshall

First published in Great Britain in 2004 by
NEW FICTION
Remus House,
Coltsfoot Drive,
Peterborough, PE2 9JX
Telephone (01733) 898101
Fax (01733) 313524

SB ISBN 1 85929 100 7

FOREWORD

When 'New Fiction' ceased publishing there was much wailing and gnashing of teeth, the showcase for the short story had offered an opportunity for practitioners of the craft to demonstrate their talent.

Phoenix-like from the ashes, 'New Fiction' has risen with the sole purpose of bringing forth new and exciting short stories from new and exciting writers.

The art of the short story writer has been practised from ancient days, with many gifted writers producing small, but hauntingly memorable stories that linger in the imagination.

I believe this selection of stories will leave echoes in your mind for many days. Read on and enjoy the pleasure of that most perfect form of literature, the short story.

Parvus Est Bellus.

CONTENTS

HOT WELCOME TO PLANET ATAU
Norman Meadows

An enemy has attacked: Planet Atau is at war! An ocean of ignited iridium flashes with brilliant orange flames as titanic waves smash upon the planet's pitted vanadium foreshores. Everywhere is riot, tumult and fury. Above the roar of battle a strident computerised voice loud-hails a warning to the earthlings daring to investigate the planet.

'I am the Grand Controller: I warn you; Our Great Programmers of the Oceans and Heavens are even now sweeping through the exit portals from the skies, bringing software for our Magic Moons. If you do not leave we shall release the seas of tunnelled silicon, making our vast lakes of mercury seethe and boil. And there will be more. Much more. Beware, you and your ways are known to us!'

As the message is not understood there is no reply. The Grand Controller issues a command: 'Load. Discharge at will.' As the deadly software is engaged the voice extends its invocations. 'Curl your sullen lips mighty rollers, defy the enemy with your spectral snarls. Dash your frightful breakers on that malignant infestation of slime-grey spaceships seeking to invest our sacred harbours. Show them the safety they think lies here is a dangerous illusion; beggar their presumptions by fire and molten metal, by the rays and malignancy of our many moonbeams, by the God of the Apocalypse! Bring annihilations - let slip the molten dogs of war. Cascade onwards great mountainous combers. Noble inheritors of our mutable spark-fired genes: destroy, destroy, destroy!'

Within the invaders' spaceships a formidable phalanx of the front row lookouts, a whole cohort of platinum-plated archaeopteryx, gasp through their heated gizzards; expiring just before a second row of defensive copper-hued hyaenadons vaporise. Assigned as the pride of Earth's upwardly evolutionary spiral, the ultimate ion revisionist DNA technology; thought to be impermeable, irresistible. Hyaenodons crafted from the most savage of their kind, bonded with double helix strands from white sharks and venomous sea snakes. The ultimate mutants, all now just cremated ashes.

The worst is yet to come. A command oscillates onwards, 'Discoverers of the Chromium trees, fire and inspire the dawn. Sweep down to join the Guardian Swordfish Puncturers flying in from the reddening east. Rise heraldic divisions of Cosmic Plunderers, raise your warding banners high. Ataurans, regard with awe those black metallic visors glinting in the flames: and beware the searing phosphors from the phasor dreamboat guns targeting the invaders' craft.

Join with me now in a mighty concourse, enhance still further our mounting power and menace, invisible yet to the proud earthlings sheltering in their self-deceiving cocoons. Abhor these aliens cloaked by leprous hides, shun their shifty elliptical eyes; inflict a myriad of debilitating pin-pricks upon them until their blood stream's moon-red. Do not let them die slowly: the watchful survivors must trace us in their brains! Infiltrate those corrugations locked in their craniums; deceitful brains, hidden from view, unreadable even to themselves. Avoid above all their only effective defensive weapon, the stench of hell exuding from their most unappealing extra terrestrial smell!'

Even before the speech is concluded, laser beams fire wildly from the spaceships' portals, towards defending creatures with jellyfish inheritance driven by a subtle and advanced hydrogen fuelled collective intelligence. Subjects of aeons of transforming mutations transcend their unfortunate visitors' wildest dreams. Acting as focussing lenses, passing the beams through protective umbrellas and trailing intestines, redirecting them back to the ships from which the rays came.

But the invaders will not be repelled without a fight: they are brave mutants - from human stock. The Fleet Admiral falls; a new Commander steps forward declaring, 'A wise man does not attempt to rip meat from an adult tiger, nor seek to steal away its young from the den while mother is there. Inheritance and enhancement will not pass unfulfilled; let our aggressive drives aggregate until manifest to the utmost, even beyond the boundaries of suicidal import. You have trained hard and long to equip yourselves to combat such a world as this, learning to wrest resources from violent opposers, fight for the last fragments. But while acknowledging the rights of owners to their possessions we reserve to ourselves the God-given rights of pre-emptive action and sequestration by force.'

Cries of, 'Yea, yea, USA,' echo and re-echo.

The new Commander continues. 'We must find out how such simple creatures can exploit non-sustainable sources in a manner we have never achieved. This will be the pinnacle of achievement for our present mission. The continued coexistence of mankind with his environment depends on this; survival, no more and no less. With these thoughts before you, gird ourselves for the fight! Deploy your battlefield weapons of mass destruction, detonate your explosive nuclear grenades, launch the photon bombs, ultimately devastate with neutrino rays.'

Spurred on the assailants' weaponry bursts upon the enemy. Seven blue moons orbiting overhead quiver in their concordant orbits, moon-wind powered vanes crumple, their daggered sails pointing aimlessly at a benighted sky. Molten seas are thrown into dangerous turbulence by the magnetic storms invoked: chaos begins to replace order. Now the Ataurans are alarmed as never before.

Responding rapidly they feed hot residues of plutonium plankton into rivulets running from their inland lakes, confluent now, forming turbulent streams of green-gold plasma. On the imploding crests of the resulting wavelets a cohort of armour-plated ships bear onwards, accompanied by a collegiate caucus of armoured krill, rising and dipping with the swell. Confusion begins to overwhelm the invaders, driven now to the most drastic measures.

The Commander responds, commanding, 'Men, from the phalanx, assemble the blaster.'

The inter-galactic wormhole super gun has never been used in anger; its dematerialising and levitating powers are only too well known. But it must be deployed even though this means aborting the mission since all the energy sources they had hoped to pirate would be destroyed, vanishing into a cloud of inter-stellar dust. Nonetheless, the situation is desperate beyond rational measure, and quite beyond their redemption. But they will take their foe down with them, in this final act of frustrated rage!

As the enemy convoy bores onwards, one by one the earthlings' ships begin to erode away. But the super weapon still holds, resting freely on a suctioning magma. Slowly, slowly, it begins to sink. Time is now totally of the essence: it is now or never. But now it is now - and never!

Without the merest whisper of sound, with no recoil or puff of smoke, the super gun fires. Within a fraction of a nano-second the whole planet and its surrounding environment evaporate. As they do so a high energy shield screens the immediate outer space remaining. To all intents and purposes the planet and its visitors are dead. Drifting towards the ultimate vanishing point at infinity. Mission unaccomplished.

But the Ataurans are prepared. Cased within their triple skins of hot fired ceramics glisten sparklets of silicon, a life form they have chosen instead of carbon: more stable, more functional, less unpredictable. Organic substances are anathema to these creatures, rejecting the electronic vagaries of degenerate carbon based organisms, mediating their own pathways through tight time bands of probability rather than the loosely defined structures we choose to think of as obeying logical laws. Their super intelligence metamorphoses.

A giant fan whirs on a remote sustainable space station. Particles of dust are suctioned in, centrifuged to separate foreign bodies, with the desired residue deposited on a nucleating energy source.

A recognisable shape evolves around the central core: within less than a second of our time a new planet appears: Atau's parallel twin.

A reconstituted Computer Control Team sets to work. Software is developed and downloaded; sophisticated interfaces evolve, interconnections grow. Vast neural nets form and the silicon lakes fractal into huge networks of bonded functional identities. A billion nerve nets encompass one thin film, these aggregate to form blocks, blocks to monumental pillars.

But no Tower of Babel is to be found here, all speak the same language, there is no learning process, only inheritance. No memory loss, no ageing. Only their lunar cells need an occasional recharge. Now firmly under computer control the whole environment is powered up, returning to its former pristine state. Set apart from all this within the Department of Pre-Historic Restoration a sealed metal bin enshrines the particles accrued as a result of the invaders' brief presence. An attached label reads: *For Processing.*

The Atauran Controller is back on line. 'Secure your capsules. Initiate the Quantum Transitioner. Begin the sequence.'

A series of pre-programmed quantum jumps drives the recreated planet back into its former position and orbit. Nothing now appears to have changed. The victors celebrate, filling their time-honoured Virtual Victor's Cup with libations, dredged up from their recuperation resort on the drugged fermenting Sea of Serendipity. Here peace, order and calm are restored. The Swordfish Puncturers and Cosmic Plunderers join the Discoverer of the Chromium Trees, enjoying their well-earned rewards of virtual reality games and contests.

With one more task to perform the Great Programmer of Oceans and Heavens alone remains on duty. The temporary force field imposed has screened all the recent activities from the distant earthlings: now return signals will be needed to compensate with complete realism for any missing gaps in Earth's received data.

Under close control the Great Programmer prepares to send back encrypted data to Earth. When it eventually arrives it will reveal information concerning planetary energy reserves, climate and the nature and disposition of its inhabitants. As the Ataurans decree.

But firstly the ashes of the earthlings and the debris of their spacecrafts must be reconstituted, the invaders brainwashed and reinstated in their former posts.

Paying every attention to detail, Atau's chemists ensure the fuel is identical to that at the moment of landing, technicians amend their logs and the computer hard and soft disc drives. Hulls of vessels are steam cleaned. No clues are left. The many different happenings have effectively never occurred.

The Great Programmer's logic circuits begin to trip, nearing depletion in attempting to draft a reply acceptable to Earth. 'Do you think this will do? We must have it exactly right, I realise that.' The creature is unusually uncertain.

Scanning a display screen carefully, the Grand Controller replies, 'Admirable. You've caught their affected air of superiority well, the tortuous phrases, their striving for dramatic effects, as well as the fractured verse. That age-old film reference is brilliant. How on Atau could such lame-brains ever have thought they would conquer *us!*'

The message is ratified by the Supreme Council of Moontalkers; congratulatory signals pulse down communication super highways, the Virtual Victor's Cup is filled to overflowing.

Worm-holed back to Earth where radio telescopes and space platforms are scanning for intelligence from outer space, the message is identified, decrypted and relayed to Exploration HQ. In a tone of evident disappointment, the Station Commander reads it out to the waiting team.

'We regret to record that Planet Atau is an inhospitable place. A most bizarre cacophony of creatures co-exist here under meagre subsistence conditions, far worse in fact that on Earth. The climate is dangerously unappealing. Storms rage, the seas are of molten metal, turbulent and destructive. Cohorts of armoured sea creatures inhabit offshore mineral or other resource development. In short, what you would find here is an inhospitable, disorganised and diabolical shambles. Our Hannibal Lecter would be no more than an underling prince among these disgusting creatures. Under no circumstances seek to colonise this brutal and declining planet; eternally dark, a menacing blot on an otherwise unblemished inter-stellar horizon. Do not be deluded into visiting this horrid heap of excrement merely because it is a reachable satellite of our nearest star.

Our nature at its worst far outweighs these alien creatures at their best, so please do not ever be so foolhardy as to try to be their uninvited guest! See you in nine years time. Exploratory Fleet Commander Wise.'

On return the brainwashed Space Fleet crews will not change one word.

AND THEY NEVER SAW HER AGAIN
Janet Cavill

I boarded the local train for the last few miles of the journey, the coaches were fairly full, but I managed to get a seat. A young man across the bay helped me to put my luggage on the rack. I sat down next to a young woman with two children. I was very tired and within a few minutes, I think I was asleep. It was an uneasy sleep and I could hear the children chattering to each other. The whole atmosphere was cosy.

The train rumbled on; as the telegraph poles flickered by with monotonous regularity, they seem to whisper, 'She was never seen again, she was never seen again.'

After a while I became aware of a little girl on the seat beside me, a rather sad looking little girl with ringlets, who snuggled up as if for warmth. Her small hand gripped my arm as she said, 'Have you seen my mummy, is she on the train?'

I said, still half asleep, 'No, she's on the ship with Susan.'

'Please help me?' she said.

Slowly as the questions I asked were answered, her story unfolded. Her father worked at the Embassy in France. The little girl, whose name turned out to be Mary, and her elder sister had remained at home with their mother - in order to be educated in England.

They had to rely on the telephone to keep up family links.

By the time the school holidays arrived, the girls had been crossing off the days on the calendar for several weeks, and arrangements were now in place for the journey to France.

They had a number of visits to town to buy new clothes and had saved their pocket money to buy their father a present. The day before their journey to France, they visited the hairdresser to have a 'trim', and did last minute shopping.

They went to bed early - and the following morning they got up equally early and had breakfast. There was laughter and fun in the bathroom, as they all had a bath and dressed, ready for their journey.

At 9.30am the taxi arrived to take them to the railway station; Mother had to go back to make sure that she had put off the gas.

They arrived at the station with time to spare and joined the queue, whilst Mother bought the ticket to Dover.

There was enough time to go to the coffee bar and buy a drink and a sticky bun. The train arrived and a porter helped them onto the train and to their seats.

Mother told the girls that there would be a dining car, which served delicious food.

The train sped along through beautiful countryside - the travellers were reading and some were sleeping. The whole journey was idyllic.

Mother had told the girls that they must not become separated - it was essential to stick together. They walked to the dining car and feasted their eyes on lovely food laid out on tables spread with beautiful white cloths.

When they reached Dover other people appeared to take over. All the luggage was collected together and placed on a conveyor belt. The girls had been mesmerised to see all the cars being transported onto the ferry. It was soon time for the family to board the ferry and they were escorted to the lounge, and Mother said that she would take them along to the saloon bar. There they would meet other families going to France to see their fathers. One family in particular was with a nanny; their mother was staying in England where she was a doctor at the local hospital. Another family had been on this journey now for three years - and really knew the 'set up' very well.

There was much socialising that afternoon; introductions were made. Everyone shook hands - and invitations were passing to everyone for lunch, morning coffee, afternoon tea and dinner; and the children got to know each other and started to play some deck games.

Mary was enjoying the crossing and she walked to the side of the ferry with the children she had just met, although their parents all appeared to know each other, and there was much name dropping.

There were warning notices all along, warning people of areas not to go to, and areas not to cross.

Mary was playing a game of deck ball, passing the ball from one to the other - there was laughter and chatter; when suddenly the ball was thrown, Mary thought that it was going overboard - and she jumped to catch it. Suddenly, and without warming, Mary had vanished - vanished into the deep blue abyss.

At that moment I became aware that the train had stopped - people were standing up and doors were being slammed.

I leaned forward and addressed the man across. 'Did you see where the little girl sitting next to me went?'

'Sorry,' he said, 'I though that you were alone.'

The woman sitting next to him confirmed what he had said.

It was impossible to believe that no one had noticed such a sweet little figure.

And yet it was as though she had . . .

MRS GARRETTY
Catherine Le Dret

Lying in bed, Mrs Garretty could hear the deep silence enfolding the house.

Snow, she thought. *It couldn't be dawn yet, could it?* She turned her head toward the luminous dial of the clock by her bedside.

5.35am. Too early. Always too early. She reached for the cane by her bed and with years of long practise, pulled the thick curtains open.

My yes, snow was over a foot deep and falling in fat, slow flakes. Drifts of snow were piling up on the kerbs and into the street. The roof to the Eberly's house was buried under its weight. She couldn't see the Whitmore's and the streetlight was dimmed through a curtain of wet snow. Everything was silent, the sounds muffled by the snow. No morning milk van to let her know someone else was awake as early as she.

The doctor will be late, she thought. She felt let down. The doctor was a friend, a former medical student with Edward. Briefly her thoughts turned to her oldest son. The young face, round and full of delight, turned upwards toward her.

'Mum, can I have . . . Mum, can I go . . . ' full of the world yet to be.

His face old now, sunken, the hands spotted with age, the face of a man too stubborn to retire. Edward, a grandfather.

If the doctor is late, will he be able to stay for a visit? They always talked a while, Doctor Lesley and she. He was being thoughtful, she knew that, but they had wonderful talks. Not about her aches and pains. There is nothing that can be done about age except the one thing no one can avoid. They talked about the world of yesterday, memories, music, beloved books. And medicine. Of course, medicine. Its progress. Its failures. Mrs Garretty was no doctor, but she was the daughter of a doctor and the mother of a doctor and soon to be the grandmother of a doctor. She remembered her father's face as a young man, bearded and serious, getting up in the middle of the night.

'It's nothing, Bertie,' reassuring his sleeping wife, 'Mrs Tanner is having her baby.' Or, 'Old Mr Poole has taken a turn for the worse.' Hitching up the horse by lantern light.

Mrs Garretty would be very disappointed if Doctor Lesley could not come. It was always 'Doctor Lesley' and always 'Mrs Garretty'.

Mrs Garretty hadn't always been Mrs Garretty, of course. She hadn't always been old, with frail white hands lying fragile on the white fold of the sheet, a face preserved in parchment, her hair was still long, still in a braid, completely white. She had never cut her hair. Once it had been the colour of August fields, rippling in the summer sun. She was Anne Cawles, born right here in this very house on Oakbridge Road. Then the house had been on the edge of town, prime farmland. Now houses stretched out in all directions, even across the river, that lovely summer river, slow and deep, and overshadowed by trees. Oak, obviously, but willows too and in the hot summer days the insects skimmed across the water top like skaters. The river was the reason her dad had stopped here when he came from the city. He bought the land, started building a house and married the farmer's daughter, almost before he put up his brass plate. There they are, Andrew and Alberta Cawles standing in front of the new horse and buggy, the photograph is old, sepia-toned. Bertie smiles proudly from her new husband's arm. Dad was a big man with a thick beard and a smile for Anne, for his patients.

Mrs Garretty watched the snow falling and the first light of dawn brighten the eastern sky, the sweep of snow.

'Drat,' she had to go. That meant the long manoeuvre to the bathroom. Legs slowly moved over the side of the bed. She pulled on her wool dressing gown, searched with her feet for her slippers on the floor. Cane in hand, she pulled herself upward and shuffle, shuffle, thunk, shuffle, down the hall, turn left. That finished, Mrs Garretty was taken with the idea of a hot bath. There was no one to stop her and, 'It's for the doctor,' she said to herself. Mrs Garretty had been severely warned about the perils of bathing alone, of falling, of broken hips, of fragile bones. But already, she was turning the knobs, steaming water filled the new, modern tub her son had insisted she have. It took a lot to get her thin bones into the water, all the way in, not sitting on a stool while the visiting nurse washed her hair, her back. How humiliating that, just like a child again. 'Oh, how lovely hot water is.'

I was pretty once, Mrs Garretty thought. Laughing at Billy Garretty, teasing him, just as they had teased each other as children.

'What makes you think I'd marry an Irishman, William Garretty?' and her laugh was full of summer sunshine and her hair caught the light.

'Because I'm the only man in your life, Annie and you know it.' William was the only one to ever call her Annie. And oh, he was so handsome.

Mrs Garretty made her way down the corridor, into the kitchen, plugged in the kettle. A nice pot of tea on a tray, some toast. She could wait for Joan to come to fix her lunch.

'Mum, Mum, Billy Garretty is in the daffodils.'

'Come on, Annie, come out and play,' Billy calls hopefully.

And Mum sighs and says, 'All right then, go out and play Anne, but stay away from the river. It's too dangerous for children. You might drown.'

But children are never afraid, so they sneak down to the river to watch the shadows through the overhanging trees, watch the insects skip across the surface of the placid currents, catch sight of an occasional fish. Billy throwing stones, throwing sticks and Anne is happy.

Proudly Mrs Garretty carried her tea tray back to her room, cane over one arm. She settled herself once more in bed, propped up with pillows and watched the dim sunlight filter through the falling snow, sipping tea, waiting for the doorbell to ring, the sound of the key, a call of, 'Hello there, Mrs Garretty, it's me, Joan.' Listening for the thump of her shoes. There never was such a nosy woman, but good-hearted and a good housekeeper. Joan loved gossip. She kept Mrs Garretty filled in on all the neighbourhood news.

'She's living with him without even being married, do you know that?' and, 'He drinks too much for his own good if you ask me, Shelby does.'

And Mrs Garretty always nodded and said, 'Hmmm,' trying not to encourage her because Mum had taught her that gossip was mean, but not wanting Joan to stop talking either. It was better than the radio.

And what does she say about me? Mrs Garretty wondered with some amusement.

'Starlight, star bright, first star I've seen tonight . . . ' they sing in their young voices.

'What do you wish Billy?'

'I want to be a sea captain and sail around the world. What do you wish?'

'Can't tell or it won't come true,' Anne says primly and truth to tell she doesn't know what she wishes for, perhaps to be Billy Garretty's best friend, but she was already. She knew that.

'Anne, Anne, it's getting dark, you come in now,' Mum's voice calls from the house.

'I got to go now Billy, really.' And Billy picks a dandelion and puts it in her hair before running away.

Mrs Garretty heard the clock chime ten o'clock in the hallway. What has happened to Joan? It was time to eat and she was tired. Soon they would come, either Doctor Lesley or Joan. Thinking about turning on the radio, she fell asleep, surrounded by the deepening snow and the silence. When she woke up again it was after twelve. The snow was slowing down some, but piled heavily in the streets. She saw the taillights of a car slide zigzag in the distance. She was hungry. Where was Joan? Mrs Garretty reached for the phone by her bed but there was no sound. She tried the radio and through the static heard warnings of heavy snow, closed schools, snarled traffic, accidents.

That's why Doctor Lesley was held up, and she knew it was unlikely she would see him that day. Again, she pulled her legs over the bed, shuffled to the kitchen, heated up soup, got some bread. How tiring. How nice to be back in bed. But it was growing colder. Mrs Garretty reached a hand toward the radiator. Yes, there was heat. She hoped the lights wouldn't go off. She couldn't possibly move again.

'William Patrick Garretty, do you take Anne Elizabeth to be your lawful wedded wife . . . '

Anne is in yards of white lace looking into the strange familiar face of William Garretty in grey tails and the dim church smells of flowers as Father Timothy pronounces them man and wife and now it is Anne's turn to feel timid. After the champagne, after the cake and the dancing and all the friends, she would go home with his man she had known all her life and did not know at all.

William, sweet William, who lifts the veil and kisses her, his lips soft and cool as the church and, *oh goodness, I hope Mum remembered to get the name cards on the table,* thinks Anne, bride of only a few moments.

Drifting in and out of sleep, time slow as the snow drifted outside, Mrs Garretty gave up hope that anyone would make it to see her that day. The room was definitely colder. Her frail hands seemed so far away. And then William is there, her sweet William, standing by the bed with a baby in his arms.

'It's a boy, Annie. A boy,' and his voice breaks with emotion. And Anne, tired out from the long hours of childbirth, takes the infant in her arms, studies his face eyes half closed, tiny hands curling and uncurling like seashells in tidewater, pulls him to her breast.

'You're a dad now William.' And she smiles before falling asleep.

In her room, Mrs Garretty couldn't seem to feel her hands and feet. Everything was very cold. Cold outside. Cold inside. She turned her head toward the window and knew it would be dark early.

Anne is kneeling in the darkened room and her grief is a pain clutching her around the middle and tears burn in her eyes, rosary in hand. Her prayer is a lamentation, 'Hail Mary, full of grace, the Lord is with thee . . . ' Oh William, dear William and she kneels all night by the open coffin and watches the waxen face that does not resemble her William at all.

'I can't go on, how can I go on without you, William?' she whispers. But that was over twenty years ago.

Mrs Garretty tugged feebly at the covers and managed to pull the knitted wool bedspread her mother had made for them, deep rose faded now, up over her feet and cold hands. She stared out the window and waited.

The snow was deep and there was no sound except the house creaking and then Billy Garretty is handing her a daffodil and calling, 'Come out Annie, come out,' and it is summer and warm and she is up and running with Billy.

Mrs Garretty's breath exhaled as slowly and cold as the winter air. In the distance a doorbell rang.

THE GREEN GATE

(For Dominic)
Amanda-Lea Manning

The boy waited impatiently, swinging to and fro on the wooden gate, chipping the green paintwork each time it hit a large granite stone jutting out from the flower bed.

The boy's face lit up when he saw his grandpa pull up in his old Rover. Running to him as he shut the car door, the boy grabbed his hand and ran alongside as they entered the house.

'Grandpa's here,' echoed through the hallway and all at once the rest of the family convened from all directions with plenty of hugs and kisses.

Lunch was to be served at 1 o'clock sharp. The table set for seven waited invitingly. Roast beef and all the trimmings was on the menu, empty plates showed much appreciation. Dessert was always popular, but the boy never indulged in sweet things, maybe he thought it too girlish.

His three siblings, all younger than he, would play their childish pranks, the boy trying hard to be grown up, would soon weaken and instigate more naughtiness. The parents would then appear telling the soaked youngsters to turn off the hose pipe, or to go and wash after throwing mud at each other, the greenhouse was always a bone of contention, the football had broken numerous panes of glass throughout the many summer times.

At the back of the house were wooded areas. The boy would sometimes slip away unnoticed, he liked to be alone sometimes, he was the oldest after all. He loved the springtime best, when all the green shoots would sprout from the trees. For hours he would lie on a mossy bank and watch the woodland creatures. Baby rabbits would dart into their burrows when danger prevailed.

On this particular day, the boy had been laying quietly, after closing his eyes once or twice he seemed to fall into a twilight sleep. He awoke with a start. His surroundings had altered dramatically. He felt cold, only dressed in shorts and a sweater. The ground was covered with snow. The trees hung heavy, their boughs weighed down by the snow.

The boy stood up amazed at the sight before him, how could this be? It was springtime. To his surprise his clothes remained quite dry. He decided he must venture home, he turned around trying to decipher the direction he had come from, but everything looked so very different. He started to walk to the left, but the snow grew deeper and the trees seemed to multiply in number. He then turned to the right becoming a little concerned, in case he could not find the green gate again.

Twenty minutes later he reached the gate. Relief was his first reaction, but the snow remained which was confusing. Was he dreaming? No, he knew he was not.

The boy opened the gate, the latch seemed different, but he carried on. The house remained the same in appearance. The gardens were more uniform, in spite of the snow he could see distant paths which lead to a centre patio. Two benches were parked opposite each other. The boy walked towards them leaving his footprints in the snow. There seemed to be a plaque on the first, he brushed away the snow and read the words 'For Alice 1815'. The boy then went to the second bench and found the words 'For James 1815'.

The boy realised that these benches were no longer a part of his garden, nor the paths or patio. Yet the house was definitely unchanged, in statue anyway. Now he was very bewildered.

The boy walked to the front door, which now sported a dark green paint and a large brass knocker. Alongside was a bell push the boy had never seen one before. He pulled it hard and jumped out of his skin when a loud bell rang above him. The door was opened by a man dressed in strange costume. The boy went inside, the man seemed unaware of him and simply closed the door again and walked off down the hall. The boy glanced upwards at the walls, which were covered in red and gold striped wallpaper. The furniture was extremely elegant. He stood in a trance-like state, what had happened to his home? Where was his family? Panic overcame him and hastily he walked into the room he knew as the sitting room. He paused at the door. He noticed two boys sitting in silence on a sofa. Their ages must have been of eight or nine years. Two adults sat separately, the man reading a journal, the woman involved in needlepoint. The light was dim, but a huge log fire flickered in the stillness. The boy was conscious of a deep sadness or maybe a family argument had ensued.

He walked towards the sofa being somewhat surprised that no one looked up or seemed to acknowledge his presence. The four seemed oblivious of him totally.

The boy noticed some framed portraits on a bureau by the window. Slowly he went to inspect them. The first was of a girl being about five years. Inscribed at the bottom of the frame was the name 'Alice'. The boy paused for a while, something about the portrait disturbed him, but he could not understand what it was. He moved to the next, a boy of about nine years gazed at him, it was also inscribed, he read 'James'. A cold shiver ran down his spine, he was looking at himself, in all but attire. The features were his own. He returned to look at the girl's portrait and it became clear, this was his younger sister's image. A fear ran through him like no other. He shook unable to comprehend anything anymore.

He turned towards the patrons and called out, 'Can you hear me, can you see me? Please answer.' The silence was deathly. It was then he realised no real harm could come to him and he regained his composure. He left the room and went to the room he knew as his dining room. Now it was floor to ceiling shelves stocked with many volumes, a library of course. Standing by the window was a desk. He wandered over noticing piles of Chronicles. Their layout seemed so antiquated, but then nothing seemed to make sense anymore. He took the first one and flicked through the pages, everything looked so obscure, the writing, the pictures. There was nothing of any relevance so he kept thumbing through each copy.

The eighth one however told him everything. Not only were there two portraits of Alice and James on the first pages but the write up that followed made him swallow hard. It appeared that the two children had fallen through the ice on Darleigh Common and drowned in 1815. This knowledge frightened the boy, the resemblance of his sister and himself in spite of their ages being older than the two lost children, didn't seem to register.

It was after all 1969, not 1815, so why did he feel so vulnerable. He must somehow get back to his home as he remembered it. The trepidation in one so young was awesome.

He ran from the library to the hall, the front door lay ahead. The boy tried to open the door. It was stuck. He then noticed a large bolt halfway up which he could not reach. He glanced around for something to stand on and pulled a chair towards the door and stood upon it releasing the heavy bolt. Removing the chair he opened the door and ran from the house through the garden. Snow still lying on the ground, his heart started pounding fast. He must get to the green gate.

At last he noticed it and almost fell onto it, darkness had fallen and he began to feel the cold as he commenced swinging on it as fast as he could. Backwards and forwards, slipping off it several times as the snow was now freezing. He held on tightly closing his eyes he spoke out loudly, 'Please God take me back to my time.' He prayed hard.

One cannot be sure how long it had been, but suddenly the boy found himself on the ground with a grazed knee. The snow had vanished completely and the temperature was much milder.

The boy noted the scuffmarks on the green gate where the paint had been chipped, this made him happy. He ran with gross impatience towards the front door calling out his sister's name.

She appeared at once and a massive relief spread over the boy like honey.

'Where's Grandpa?' he asked smiling smugly.

'It's 8.30pm, he had to leave, where have you been? We have been calling you for ages,' his mother entreated in a rather miffed fashion.

The boy smiled again realising he had been there all the time, simply in a different dimension, but who would believe him?

THE PICTURE
T G Bloodworth

It was one of those shops, antique, curio, second-hand, junk, call it what you will, where I found it. The picture itself was pleasant, a landscape, nothing outstanding, but the frame was what took my eye. It had the appearance of solid gold, ribbed like a Cornish pasty. Dull in colour, yet I knew I had to have it. £15 seemed a bit extravagant, but no doubt the shopkeeper would make a handy profit. It seemed old in design, possibly Victorian, probably from a house clearance somewhere local. I was in Bournemouth for a weekend away. Single, unattached, 28 but happy in myself, content with life, not yet having found someone to settle down with.

My home was in the Cotswolds, a small cottage about 20 minutes from Gloucester, easily accessible thanks to the motorways. Being self-employed, an accountant by trade, there were plenty of small businesses in the area, especially in the Stroud Valley.

Returning with my purchase to the hotel, I placed the picture where I could see it from the bed. After dinner and a few drinks I decided on an early night and a good book. It was Sunday tomorrow, mid September, most shops would be open for the end of the holiday season. It was gone 11pm before I put the book down with a yawn, sleep was at hand. Lights out and I was deep in slumber.

Not sure what time it was, I awoke with a start, only the odd streetlight confirmed it was still night. Then I froze, an old lady stood by the wall, holding my picture. She looked at me as if pleading for help, but I was terrified. Gradually I found my voice, 'What do you want?' was all I could manage, but she made no reply. Just pointed at the picture, then placed it back against the wall and promptly disappeared. Not sure that perhaps it was all a dream, I put the light on. The picture was where I had placed it, nothing appeared out of place. Too many drinks I thought, turning the light out, back to sleep!

Next morning I showered and shaved ready for a good breakfast. I sat on the bed, putting my shoes on, as I did I glanced at my painting with a wry smile. Then I went cold again, mesmerised, the picture was upside down. It seemed like an age before I moved, as I turned the picture round, something caught my eye. It appeared to be some very small writing, almost hidden by the shadow of the frame.

After breakfast I took a stroll along the sea front still thinking about my strange experience. I came upon a street market. Always looking for a bargain I wandered around. A small magnifying glass caught my eye. *Just the job,* I thought, remembering the writing on the picture. £2 well spent. I was leaving for home later in the day, so after lunch I packed my case all ready to go.

Using the magnifying glass, I examined the back of the picture. It looked like an address, 16 Baker Street or was it 16 Barber Street? I rang room service asking for a street guide just in case. Sure enough, there was a 16 Barber Street. There and then I decided to visit it on my way home.

I had the picture flat on the back seat of my car, eventually finding 16 Barber Street. *Now what,* I thought, something drove me on. I knocked on the door. A chap about my age answered the door. I introduced myself and explained about the picture. For a small moment I thought I had wasted my time, but then he smiled. 'Could I see the picture?' he asked.

Once he had seen it, he asked me in. Apparently the picture had belonged to his grandmother, though she had never lived at this address. His name was Robert - it seemed a coincidence that we shared the same name. As I was about to leave, the front door opened and in walked a vision of loveliness. She was Robert's sister, Samantha, for me it was love at first sight.

All three of us chatted, discussing the events that had brought us together. Of course I hadn't mentioned the 'old lady', for fear of giving the wrong impression. Time was passing all too quickly for me, as Samantha produced a photograph album. Searching quickly she gave a cry, 'Here's Grandma's picture,' but I knew before she showed me it was the 'old lady'.

Addresses and telephone numbers were exchanged. I asked Samantha if I could see her next time I was down. She nodded and said she'd like that. I took my leave and drove home.

After many phone calls and weekend trips, Samantha and I got engaged. Robert was delighted and we married a year later.

I'd never mentioned my experience in the hotel, but on returning from honeymoon we thought 'our picture' should have pride of place in our bedroom. A pleasant reminder of what brought us together.

Some weeks later, something woke me one night. Samantha was sound asleep and breathing normally. Once my eyes had adjusted to the gloom, I saw the 'old lady' standing by our picture. She nodded and gave me a lovely smile. Reassured I now know what fate was. In this case preordained happiness. That was the last time I saw the 'old lady', and never ever told a soul of the experiences!

DARK SHADOW
Kathleen Townsley

Drawing the curtains she took a last look out of the kitchen window, and felt the hairs on the back of her neck begin to rise, she quickly drew the curtains. If she had waited just a few seconds more she would have seen the dark shadow cross the bottom of the garden. Now it was too late, the final fifty minutes of her life had begun.

Shelly ran her bath, a habit she had always known: bath, evening meal, feet up and relax with the video she had been longing to see. Gently she lowered herself into the steaming water, sucking in a deep breath as the heat rose up her back, placing the pillow behind her head, she settled down to a long soak. The radio was playing beside the bath and she was humming along to her favourite tune of the week, the evening meal was warming slowly in the oven and all was right in her world.

Suddenly she sat up. 'What was that?' she said, turning the radio off she listened intently. All remained quiet.

Downstairs the dark shadow stopped its movement as the radio stopped playing. It remained still and unmoving till the music began again. Then the shadow commenced its ascent of the stairs. Shelly finished bathing and stepped out of the bath, reaching for the towel, hand outstretched she stopped. This time there was no mistake, someone was in the house. The creak on the stairs was unmistakable. Listening intently she called, 'Is anyone there?' No answer, all remained silent. Quickly she grabbed her robe, wrapping it around her tightly she slowly opened the bathroom door. The shadow heard her call out and moved behind the bedroom door. Shelly stepped onto the landing and called again, 'If there is anyone here, go now before the police arrive. I have just phoned them.'

The shadow smiled, the phone lines were dead. Walking slowly to her bedroom keeping her back pressed to the wall, all her senses alert to any sound, she entered her bedroom and slammed the door closed. The shadow smiled at her and plunged the knife in deep. For the next hour he worked without thought till his masterpiece was complete.

'Shelly, I'm home,' called Duncan, 'the meeting finished early, so I can watch that film with you. Something smells good, hope there's enough for two.' Wandering into the kitchen he switched the kettle on and began to set the table. The rose he had brought on his way home he placed on her plate. *One year today since we met,* he thought, then turning he headed up the stairs. *Maybe I can wash her back.* The bathroom was empty, the water was still sitting in the bath but he knew it was cold. Fear began to travel up his spine. Something was wrong. He called out, 'Shelly!' All remained quiet. Walking towards the bedroom he saw the lamp burning through the partially open door. 'I called but you must not have heard me . . .' the rest of the sentence died in his throat at the scene before him. He backed away from the room and turning, vomited over the banister rail. As he sank to his knees he howled in grief. The shadow smiled and moved away from the wall directly below the bedroom window, walked to the far end of the garden and walked away.

Duncan was sitting in an armchair when the police arrived, staring into space. Mr Greenwood, the neighbour said, 'This is how he has remained since he stumbled through our front door, not a word has he spoken, apart from Shelly. I have not gone next door. Judging by Duncan's face I am sorry to say I am afraid to. I just called you instead.'

The detective constable said, 'It's all right sir, I will go and see what the problem is after a few words with your neighbour.' Kneeling down he said, 'Duncan, can you tell me what happened?'

Duncan never moved, the horror on his face was enough to send the constable next door. On entering the house he saw all was quiet. The lounge was empty and the kitchen was ready for their meal. Once upstairs he entered the bedroom first. There being a light on in that room, that scene would remain with him till his dying day. The lady was stretched out on the bed, her arms were bent and the hands were nailed to each side of her head. Her eyes had been gorged out, and her mouth had been sealed tight with glue. The tube was lying by her head. On the wall above the bed writing in blood was, *see no evil, hear no evil, speak no evil.* Quickly he left the house taking gulping breaths in the evening air. He phoned for back up.

The murder hunt was in full swing when the second call came through, Again it was a young woman found by her husband at 10.30pm on his return from the 2 till 10 shift at the large car plant. No sooner had that left the headlines when call three arrived. This one was different, this time it was a man.

At the briefing the inspector said, 'I now have the profile report in front of me and I will try to explain the reasoning behind these three murders according to our expert . . .' who sitting at the back of the room nodded his acknowledgement, 'the three horrific murders are identical in each case, but if you reverse the order they were found you will see a pattern evolving. Murder victim number three had a nail through each eye, while number two had a row of nails, five to be exact, hammered into the mouth, that being the only difference, for the rest of the injuries remain the same. This leads the expert to suggest, Shelly, victim number one, heard the evil, victim number three, Fiona, saw the evil, whilst number two, David, spoke the evil. As we know they all worked for the same car plant. Whatever occurred must have been at the plant for they never socialised outside of working hours. Therefore the main area to look at is the stores, for whatever occurred there was seen by Fiona, then when Shelly came down to the stores for office equipment, Fiona passed on the information to her, she in turn told her boss David when she returned to the office. He must have gone to see the murderer, and that sealed all their fates, so I will divide the room into halves. Half of you here will re-interview everyone who works in stores, the rest will tear that place apart.'

The interviews began just after 10am. As lunchtime approached everyone who worked in stores had been seen. The storeroom was a mess but nothing was found, they had to admit they have drawn a blank.

Duncan was sitting in the lounge several months later, going over the letter he had received from the investigator telling him he had at last found something to his advantage. Shelly's murderer he knew would be caught and sent to jail for the rest of his life, but he wanted to reek his own revenge first. It had taken months, but he had remained patient and now it looked like he had finally been given a break. He would contact him immediately. He heard a noise coming from upstairs, climbing the stairs two at a time he stopped outside the bathroom door. Water was seeping under the door. Quickly he went inside and saw the bath overflowing. Thinking he had started to run a bath then forgot, he turned off the taps and quickly went to the airing cupboard to grab some towels to soak up the water. As he knelt down the shadow moved, before Duncan could turn round he felt a blow to the back of his head. On opening his eyes he realised he was lying on his bed, trying to sit up, the room began to spin, and the pain in his head became intense.

Duncan lay still, then he saw movement from the corner of his eye. The shadow stepped forward, raising its arm high. Duncan immediately saw in its hand was a large hammer. He tried to scream but no sound came out. The shadow swung the hammer and began to hammer the first nail into Duncan's head. Mercifully after the first nail entered his skull Duncan fainted and never woke to feel the remaining eleven hammered deep into his skull.

Mr Greenwood saw the front door standing open and shouted out to Duncan. On getting no response he entered. Water was pouring down the stairs. Without thought he ran up the stairs and straight to the bathroom. Fearing the worst, he burst through only to find the bath empty. Releasing his breath with a sigh, he felt the relief wash over him. He had feared for Duncan, the poor man was still grieving for Shelly. Heading back toward the top of the stairs something caught his eye. What he cannot say to this day, but it made him turn towards the bedroom. That is when he fainted. The shadow stepped over the man's body and walked down the stairs, out of the back door, without a backward glance. As Mr Greenwood opened his eyes he remained lying on his back. Something told him not to stand and look round. What the reason was he did not recall. Rolling onto his hands and knees he crawled to the top of the stairs. All he knew was he had to get away, and get help.

The police arrived and found written above the bed in blood these words, *evil thinkers.* Forensics were soon on the scene. They did not hold out much hope of fingerprints, but they tried anyway. The inspector was standing in the bedroom when his sergeant handed him an evidence bag. 'This was found on the coffee table in the lounge, no envelope, which means it was pushed through the gentleman's door.' The inspector read the short note.

'Dear Duncan, I think I have a break through at last, please phone as soon as you receive this note. Reginald Browning'.

Quickly the name was put through the main police computers and it was soon found to be a Reginald Browning private investigator, a police car was despatched immediately to the address. The inspector received the call to say the man had been found barely alive, and was at this moment being rushed to the hospital. When the inspector arrived at the hospital the constable immediately told him what he had found. Mr Browning's door was open and on entering found Mr Browning face down on the bed, his tongue having been cut out and nailed to the headboard, several nails had been hammered into his back, above the bed was written in blood, *evil doer.* Mr Browning was at this time undergoing major surgery.

It was several days later when the full extent of his injuries came to light. As the inspector sat in the consultant's office that evening he learnt the truth. The man was paralysed from the upper chest down, unable to speak, or move any part of his body. This ruled out any chance of him being able to put into writing the evenings of that night, and as the doctor continued, it became clear that due to the ordeal the consultant was not certain if he had maintained a sound mind, so in their opinion Mr Browning would never do anything again. As for an interview, that too was dismissed by them.

The inspector left the hospital deep in thought unaware that a shadow followed close behind, in the gloom of the car park. As the inspector climbed into his car and drove away, the shadow smiled and melted into the night, safe from discovery.

BAD HAIR DAY
Anne Rolfe-Brooker

Actually, the day had begun rather badly for Geoffrey Budkins, but in that mish mash of unhappy circumstances, there had been nothing to indicate that the day would end with him being abducted by aliens.

His initial mistake had been getting out of bed at all, and his second mistake had been sliding on his slippers while still half asleep, and not noticing that Archie, the red ginger tomcat he had saved from drowning as a kitten, had performed his toilet in the left aforesaid article of footwear.

The morning post did little to alleviate his mood, containing as it did a tax demand for some few thousand pounds, backdated to the days when he had tried his hand at running a taxi business (which failed) and a final demand for the electricity bill to be paid, carrying the somewhat disconcerting threat that if it were left unpaid for seven days from the date of the letter, Geoffrey would be without power. Glancing at the heading of the paper, he observed that the date of the letter was eight days ago, a favourite means of aggravation employed by most utility companies, showing that clerks and bureaucrats do have a sense of humour, albeit rather black.

The third and last envelope he opened contained the following cryptic message: *Budkins, pack your clothes for Mars. Dress warmly.* It was signed 'A Friend'.

Geoffrey glanced at the fat-spattered calendar above his cooker. It was definitely the end of October, *too early,* he thought, *for an April fool's day joke.* He tried to tear up the card, but found it impossible to do, so he tossed it into the swing bin and promptly forgot about it.

On arrival at his office he found that he had, as usual, forgotten to put the clocks back and was called into Mr Mears' office, where a lecture on tardiness was delivered with stentorian severity.

The afternoon passed uneventfully enough, with the exception of slightly mutilating his left index finger in the office guillotine, and tripping over the fax machine cable, thus falling and banging his nose on Tilly Branwaite's desk, producing what appeared to be copious bloodstains on her pile of typing, which in turn produced a stream of language from the girl which would have shocked a Billingsgate fish wife, had one been present.

Geoffrey had been commanded to work late, to make up the hour lost in the morning, and it was near to eight o'clock when he finally switched off the office lights, and began to move towards the door. However, something at the window, some slight movement, or perhaps luminosity, made him turn his head in that direction. He was startled to see what appeared to be a shining green gnome looking in at him.

Being of a somewhat phlegmatic disposition, Geoffrey stifled the scream, which lurked perilously close to the surface, and shut his eyes for the count of ten, his heart doing a violent Spanish flamenco inside his chest.

Bracing himself, he then opened his eyes, and was much relieved to find that the apparition had vanished. He felt as though a drink was called for and locking the office carefully behind himself, made his way to the nearest pub, aptly named The Green Spirit. Four whisky and sodas later he felt able to face the world again, and had successfully convinced himself that what he had seen had been a trick of the light, and nothing more.

Unfortunately his bravado faced another gruelling challenge as he walked through Darden Street towards his house at the end of a cul-de-sac, when a small red creature with enormous green eyes and a tail, barred his path and began to jog around in what could only be described as an enthusiastic fashion.

Geoffrey leaned against the nearest garden fence, which unhappily had not been properly maintained for a decade, and fell through it into a rose thicket, where he lay, scratched and sore, for about two minutes. This was the amount of time he needed to compose himself sufficiently to continue his walk home, but alas, as he rose to his feet, tenderly pulling out thorns from various parts of his anatomy, he became aware of the fact that he was not alone.

Small creatures, about 20 in number, were dancing round him like Dervishes; some were red, some green and some a peculiar mixture of mauve and yellow, but the aesthetic effect was lost on Geoffrey, who now passed out, falling once again into the rose bushes.

He was awoken by the coldness of a metal object being inserted into his left nostril, at which point he decided that unconsciousness was the better part of valour, and promptly passed out again. What had caused this fortunate release into near coma had been the sight of various little beings grouped around him, each with a different article reminiscent of surgical tools, jostling for a closer look at his nose, a commodity which they themselves appeared not to have.

Indeed, in his mercifully brief excursion into wakefulness, it had appeared to Geoffrey that the only 'normal' feature they possessed were eyes, although somewhat larger and deeper green than he had ever seen grace the features of a human.

When he woke again, sometime later, he was shocked to see what appeared to be a blue blob with the statutory large green eyes staring at him. He took some consolation from the fact that the hordes had departed, presumably on some questionable 'other duties'.

The blue blob spoke, in a voice that seemed to wrap every syllable with a bubble, and every pause with a sharp intake of air, though through which particular organ it breathed, Geoffrey shuddered to think. 'You got my letter?' it said, more as an accusation than a question, but then the finer nuances of the English language are frequently lost to the English, let alone an alien.

By this time Geoffrey's mind had accepted the fact that this was really happening, as the alternative was too awful to contemplate. Eccentricity played a large part in his family background, but to the best of his knowledge, there had been no definite diagnosis of insanity. This strangely comforted him.

'Oh that,' he said dismissively, remember the virtually indestructible card in the morning post. The blue entity seemed to puff up to twice its original size, thus giving the definite impression that it was not happy.

'Well, if you get pneumonia don't blame us,' the small blue creature said sniffily, and Geoffrey thought somewhat self-righteously. 'You are going to temperatures equivalent to your Siberian winters. We may be able to borrow some clothes from the humans already there, but I warn you, they're a selfish lot, like all homo sapiens, and I cannot guarantee that they will share with you.'

'Excuse me,' Geoffrey said belligerently, when the little blob had finished bubbling and burbling, 'but I am not going anywhere with you.'

He struggled to sit up on the wooden slab, but found that his arms and legs had been tied down too securely for him to move much.

At this point, a furry white creature, some two feet tall, entered and spoke in seeming gibberish to the blue blob, who listened for a moment, and then dismissed it with an impatient wave from a long claw that appeared suddenly from its jelly-like body, and which disappeared equally quickly into the blue mass.

'I am afraid you have no choice,' it gurgled smugly. 'We have arrived on Mars.'

'How did you get my address?' Geoffrey queried.

The blob blinked. 'We picked you out of your race's telephone books,' it said.

'Why me?' Geoffrey shouted. 'Why me? Why me?'

The blue blob turned and made a clicking noise, upon which a door appeared in the far wall, and opened silently. 'Why not?' he bubbled. 'Why not? Why not?' and so saying, he passed through the door leaving Geoffrey on his own to contemplate the vagaries of fate . . .

LIBERTY AND PASSION
James Stephen Cameron

Miss Emma Anne Larkin came from her walk in the beautiful summer gardens, after observing the walled kitchen area of the great house in Leicestershire, with all the marvels and wonder to be seen. Especially the man-made rectangle pond, with plenitude, teaming with carp, goldfish, tadpoles, newts, dragonflies, all busy within their small creative universe.

By this time, I was busy writing my morning's correspondence and letters, which were numerous and time consuming, but it had to be done efficiently. Come what may, a stickler for hard work with credulous performance, I dabbed my quill into the black ink, whilst thinking and pondering of my visitor's short venture within the large palatial gardens. I was daydreaming, sequestered and remote, away from the turbulent chaotic world, with moments of divine feelings that were apt to creep up on one's spirit at times of reflection. She came, smelt and placed the plucked white and red roses down upon the marble table-top near to my writing slope. The essence of the flowers made one feel divinely privileged, with sweet aromas wafting through the atmosphere invisibly. Invested with Madame's presence, triumphantly she mused, tempting me with all her natural beauty. A unique phenomena of one's heart. The chemistry was unique, and inspiring, enough to warrant further investigation. Our conversation was light-hearted and gay rightly enough. But the rebels of France were active in their wanton struggle for a republic, based on that one word, liberty, which represented freedom from a royalist monarchy. Had Robespierre gone completely mad with his unique rhetoric in making those poor ignorant wretches confess to crimes they had not even committed?

I had been an English government spy for these last three hard years, working undercover where danger was commonplace, where capture had been fraught with many obstacles, leaving me prominently scared to the eventual outcome, my arrest or death at the hands of mischievous republican dogs who were hell bent on using the guillotine to rid themselves of all aristocratic families in their midst. While the French revolution screamed liberty far too often. For now I was safe and secure, away from the tremors of the earth. April was here, the best month of the year with all her fertile abundance, where I spied the lady of my dreams.

It was while I was at the mask ball the previous night where I guessed at all her mannerisms, with my observations which were carefully kept in check, her demeanour like that of a Greek goddess, whilst my head was filled with romance. With the door to my heart open wide, with many collective thoughts to where it would all lead, my longing heart filled with palpitations. I had stood patiently holding my glass of Madeira, watching and looking, searching for those little telltale incidents that gave one permission to smile back at a suitable suitor. I could not remain in agony any longer than was necessary to my awaited fate.

I, a tyrant of love and all its complexities, surprises, rejections, happiness and unhappiness that came with its unforeseen package. I knew this child of Heaven from years before. I had played with, watched her gay, lively spirit when I was but a simple child of innocence. As we both explored the vast landscape of the house and grounds, idyllically dreaming of what adults did when they were fully grown and matured. And now, she was like an orchid, maturing and blossoming into a fine English girl. I had often admired her, secretly, with her natural blonde hair done in ringlets, and a fair sweet complexion that sent shivers down my spine. I had loved her from then, the moment my eyes were transfixed upon an endearing child of the universe. With her acute tastes for adventure, her inquisitive mind always asking questions, followed by other questions that left one drained at times. I could ill afford a refusal, at best a denial of my true feelings for this remarkable woman of society. My emotions bled with pain and heartache.

Later that morning a letter arrived from France, from my dearest cousin, Marguerite, coded of course, telling me of her troubles and all the nastiness of Paris. More unfortunates were being dragged through the cobbled streets, and the King and Queen's lives were in danger. How could I stop this madness across the English channel from happening any further, a nightmare that would not go away entirely? I had done all within my power, but it seemed inadequate and futile, it was just simply not enough. I was disturbed for the love of two females. Decision time. Mentally, my poor heart was split in two. Mental anguish set in leaving no room for error or pretence. Oh that word pretentious, where one's actions became insincere, illusions of fantasy and lies. My previous liaisons and experiences plagued my mind with lingering doubt and confusion at times. I had to nurture love without misconduct spoiling the reproach. Would another admirer beat me to it, or would I simply die with my inner thoughts? The opportunity of love was not to be missed. I had always been a lucky devil so far, inasmuch I had evaded the pitfalls of rejection, where some poor souls had committed suicide from lack of understanding that their loved one had finally brought the curtain down, extinguishing all thoughts of renewal. Incredibly I had the advantage of continuing this episode in my life with a good amount of persuasion, where liberty and passion went hand in hand. I finished my return letter to Marguerite by writing 'au revoir' twice and signed, 'I, yours forever,' at the bottom of the page, and continued to wax the envelope with my family seal. Candidly, Lady Emma asked whom it was addressed to.

'Oh, it is my sweet cousin in France. You do remember her, Emma, when we were children? I fear for her safety a million times over.'

'Yes, my Lord! Oh poor Marguerite, it is unfortunate, this awful business in Paris and her many districts which has seen the best heads fall into that common basket of death far too many times already,' said Madame, ruefully.

I fully digested her important thoughts. My heart was mellow and restrained. Times were changing with rebellion afoot across the frontiers of Europe, and here in England the government was on the edge from the doctrines of antagonists, pamphleteers, libertines, free thinkers and those who saw fit to remove all trace of the royal family once and for all. Of course it was outrageous to the extremes of fairness and good strong government. My poor heart went out to Louis and Marie Antoinette and her dear, beloved children a thousand times.

'Is Mama not about the house this fine April morn?' inquired Emma soothingly.

'No, Emma my dear. She's gone to Leicester with her charitable duties,' said I, attentively. 'We are quite alone in the library. I've informed the staff previously to leave me be until I instruct otherwise,' I continued.

She came closer behind my person and fiddled with a lock of black hair upon my head. I duly felt her presence, her soul, her heart beating away. I had not been this close in years.

'So we are totally alone, free from disturbance, my Lord. Free to say and do as we please,' declared Emma invitingly.

I said yes to nearly every word she spoke. Sweet memories filtered into my mind once again, with an inner voice commanding silently within my heart. *Take the initiative, be bold and daring.* I automatically stood back from my chair whilst sweeping her into my arms, within an embrace made in Heaven. I was immortalised with love, the very embodiment of love and its many devices. I slowly cupped my hands around her face and spoke lovingly and excitedly. All nervous energy left my happy spirit in that one single moment of time. We both kissed and pecked each other some seconds, not totally believing that we were at last together. Freedom and liberty crossed my mind. Her acceptance of me was beautifying, where I held her small waist firmly and manly. Two songbirds united in an intimate bond, our relationship made with a binding contract between two deserving people who yearned secretly for undying love. With the unique smell of lavender, her make-up was divine. Prudence would be our saviour in the long term, and mama would undoubtedly be pleased to know that we had finally made that commitment, a longing that was long overdue. Now the world felt good again, we both felt ecstatic, on top of things. The bedroom would have to wait, this to me was unimportant, nothing could exchange these intimate feelings, no gold or diamond on earth could ever do that. I allowed her head to fall upon my shoulders a while longer. Outside I viewed temporally through the French windows a variety of different bird species coming and going, singing and chirping merrily with the gracious air of spring in the room.

'Oh Dominique, it has been a long time for this to happen between us both. How I have longed for a stronger bond to develop. I may have given you the wrong impressions on occasions. A little flirting doesn't hurt. They say patience comes to those who wait. And God knows, we have both waited years and years, my sweet man. The freedom to express freely all our heartfelt desires.'

'Yes darling, the feeling is mutual and long lasting. We must both develop this love with creative input and conduct. It is not a coincidence, or silly pride interfering.' I kissed her eyes, then her temple again. This wasn't infatuation, but meaningful love at its best configuration.

Two months elapsed with important news concerning my dear cousin. Somehow she had managed to escape from all the upheavals of republican France, undetected with regard to its great network of spies, leaving behind her a trial of espionage, blabbermouths, rogues and traitors. She had been a fearless woman, credited with many moonlight adventures, braving adversity which the fairer sex would normally avoid like the plague. Her carriage and chaise arrived at the front of the colonnade and entrance to the house. Footmen soon relieved her of her baggage and hat boxes, bringing them inside the house, whilst Madame came smartly into the ante-room. Papa and Mama soon met their niece adoringly, but for me, this meant betrayal of sorts. Fundamentally I had unwittingly given my heart to another, both equally attractive in nature. What was one to do with this predicament now, I wondered? Would she call me a cheat and a liar? Were all those dear letters that I sent all meaningless, filled with conceit and misunderstanding? My territory now seemed less exciting, daunting, almost tense. My heart shivered with pretence. How would I explain myself, was the question.

Two days later, my dear cousin became suspicious and confronted me in the green dining room. Would I really confess to my inadequacies there and then? I was soon to find out from my misconduct rightly enough.

My dear cousin Marguerite fell about me, scratching, tearing away at my face in tears. 'How could you, Dominique, deny me of all people the love that is owed to me, especially as I have come home to England to stay from the long hardship and continual war. I see you in the arms of another, whom lets you with her torturous heart.;'

'I needed respite, respectively of her assumptions,' declared I, ashamedly.

'So Emma has been busy behind my back, soothing you with notions of love in my absence. What charade have you been hiding from me? Do you wish me dead, never to return from France, so you could be married with no strings attached? I must have been stupid to believe that one day you would have been mine, mine alone. Do you hear me Dominique?'

I replied with 'yes' and nearly died.

THE LOVERS
Alma Montgomery Frank

Sally Simpson was a newcomer in the pretty town of Merton in the Yorkshire Dales; little did she know that a real lasting romance was about to begin!

She gazed out of her flat window in Peach Street. It was evening and the sun was going down. Sally thought, *Peach Street is the right name for this street, especially I shouldn't wonder on an evening in the summer such as tonight's.*

Sally never knew her parents. She had been left with her gran whilst they were on holiday abroad. They never returned. Gran had lived to be quite old and had left her an adequate sum in her will. Sally felt her gran had done her proud.

Sally sold her gran's house in Oldfield and having looked around different places, Merton took her fancy. Peach Street was a must!

There was no need for Sally to rush into getting another job until she was ready but somehow, and she couldn't think why, to work again seemed to be the rule of the day.

The three agencies Sally tried in the town. Her CV qualifications were more than adequate, but each time, she had no reply. The internet wasn't much help. Sally was reading one evening the local rag when she espied an advert asking for someone with good abilities. She immediately replied to the advert having rung the phone number. A very pleasant man's voice answered the phone call and a meeting was arranged on mutual ground, The Royal Hotel in the centre of Merton. Sally had always been a person, and early bird, for an appointment, so she sat calmly in a chair in the foyer after having a word with the receptionist.

'A Mr Foley will be here shortly, Miss.'

Sitting quietly, Sally pondered inwardly. What would Mr Foley be like? From his voice on the phone she imagined he would be small but well-built, with spectacles. She couldn't have been more wrong!

A person approached the receptionist, 'Yes Mr Foley, the person sitting in the chair is Miss Simpson.'

A tall, willowy, handsome man approached Sally and said, 'I'm Michael Foley, you rang me yesterday.'

'Yes, Mr Foley.'

'I have been lent room 23 to interview you, would you like to come this way please.'

Sally hesitated for a moment thinking, *is it wise to go to a room with a stranger?* Sally noticed his eyes were twinkling with merriment.

'Come Miss Simpson, my intentions are honourable. I only wish to interview you, I take it you have your CV with you?'

'Yes, Sir,' replied Sally.

Meekly she walked along with Michael Foley to room 23. Opening the door, Michael stood aside for Sally to enter, then entered himself and quietly closed the door.

'Please sit down in the chair Miss Simpson. I will perch on the double bed.'

Sally handed him her CV and waited for the usual explosion. It did not come.

Instead, after he had read the contents, 'Well Miss Simpson, you are a well qualified person. I'm not sure my position will be what you are wanting.'

Michael Foley's face seemed to change from a stern employer to a somewhat kinder and tender man. Sally felt a little afraid yet, somehow, she knew he would not harm her.

'I'm an archaeologist and spend most of my life looking for ancient treasures wherever they may be found. I enjoyed searching for treasure in Peru last year and brought home wonderful masterpieces for the British Museum. I do need a lady to cook my meals and those of my associates, and occasionally come along and do some exploring with us. You will not be the only female. Three of my friends always bring their women along. They will take turns to do the cooking, it keeps them sane, so to speak! My new exploration is in Portugal and I thought it would be nice to have a female of my own to go with us this time. I can assure you there will never be a dull moment and the excitement of finding treasure will overwhelm you. We usually spend six months at a time, we are always not allowed any longer at a site.'

Sally had always longed to do a job quite different from office work. She looked at Michael Foley and knew she couldn't refuse working for him. 'I'll take the job. I have never cooked on a primus stove out in the open. I will do my best. When do I start please?'

Michael Foley's eyes shone with brilliance. 'Oh, thank you. Can you be ready to go to Portugal in a week's time? But, before that, I would very much like to entertain you at The Mermaid Restaurant to brief you on what to expect when we arrive in Portugal, and it will be nice to meet later, Sheila Wedgwood, Stella Millar and Joan Ovett.'

Sally was intrigued to see Michael Foley waiting at the table in The Mermaid for her. He looked immaculate in his black and grey pin-striped suit. She was so glad she had put on her best suit, a black and white affair. Her complexion and pretty long wavy fair hair, she could see pleased Michael Foley.

Michael arose from his seat and shook hands with Sally. 'Dead on time, thank you.'

During a splendid meal, Michael Foley told her what to take with her on the expedition and they would meet again at Sally's home. She noticed how charmingly he looked at her. Sally herself began to realise that Michael Foley could mean quite a lot to her in the future. He took her home in his Merc, went with her to her front flat door and taking her hand, kissed it and said, 'Goodnight Miss Simpson, please be ready with your rucksacks when I call for you on Monday, 3.30pm. We all meet at the terminal at Dover.'

The time seemed to race away but Sally had made full arrangements with her bank manager to keep paying her numerous debits. When the time came, Sally was ready waiting with undue excitement. Michael knocked on her door. Sally stood before him. 'I'm ready sir.'

'Please call me Michael.' He took her rucksacks, placed them over his broad shoulders and away they went. They greeted his friends at Dover and they made their way to Portugal.

Sally found the other ladies very pleasant and felt they would be her friends. At the Portugal site, Sally also found the other ladies as Michael had mentioned, slept with their menfolk. Michael put Sally's tent close to his in case she became frightened during the night.

One night a week later, Sally became very frightened and arose from her tent bed and called Michael's name. He was awake in a flash as though he was expecting Sally to call!

He poked his head out of his tent and said, 'What's the matter Sally?

'I'm sure I heard an alarming noise. I have heard it several times before but tonight, I couldn't sleep for it was louder than ever.'

'We have a big day in front of us tomorrow, we are quite near to the treasure we are seeking.' Michael walked into Sally's tent, picked up her bed and put it into his own. 'Come on in, I won't molest you. I have grown very fond of you Sally and I have the feeling you like me too. I have noticed you look fondly at me when I come in for meals in our food tent.'

Sally walked in and lay down on her bed. Thinking inwardly as she closed her eyes, *people do make love out of wedlock these days.*

She fell off to sleep quite happily and in the morning, Michael kissed her on her sleepy lips and merrily said, 'Time to get up, my dear.'

From that night onwards in Portugal, Sally and Michael's hearts entwined and like the other lovers, Sally spent the rest of her life seeking buried treasure with Michael and his friends. They became partners in every way for life!

LOVE'S IN-LAWS
M Webster

Helen adjusted the pillows and pulled her knees towards her, to make sitting on the bed more comfortable. The 'happy memories' box of her daughter Charlotte's life, lovingly stored for twenty-two years, lay open beside her. Helen read slowly through the letters written by Charlotte over a two-month period, while she was at college. They built up a picture of a growing romance.

'Mum, I have a new boyfriend . . .'

'. . . you would think I had known him forever.'

'. . . I think I was destined to meet him . . .'

'It's amazing, we feel the same way!'

Helen had gradually felt the need for caution. She had known the embrace of love as a student, and the hurt of rejection. Charlotte was so similar to her. They shared the birth sign Gemini - the twins. She didn't want them to share the same pain. But Charlotte had countered Helen's anxieties with greater assurance.

'You *must* see him, Mum,' she had written. 'I bet you fall for him too!'

Charlotte had sent a photo of 'Danny'; it had almost stopped her heart. Remembered dark eyes and an unforgettable broad smile beamed out at her. The photo was labelled *Daniel Gilmour* aged 21 years. But this was the face of *Patrick* Gilmour, as Helen remembered him years before!

Helen lowered herself onto the pillow and closed her eyes. Her mind travelled back to when similar brown eyes to those had stared at her across a crowded bar. She had twice looked away, before turning and holding his stare. She laughed softly at the memory of his first words. 'Would you like a crisp?'

Patrick Gilmour was different to anyone else she had met in the two years she had been at college; so serious, so caring and courteous. His gentle ways had often made her laugh, and despite her friends' opposition, they became 'an item'. However, she had a serious flaw to *her* character that Patrick was made too aware of. She had always been a flirt, and once she felt safe in their relationship, she had played her teasing game. She asked for 'space' once too often, and in the void, Patrick had met Simone.

Helen opened her eyes. The memory of her own actions had prompted her to phone Charlotte. The words she should have said ached in her throat as agony swept through her, but how could she explain to her daughter that this wonderful boy was the son of the only man she herself had loved - and lost? She hadn't told her. She merely poured a mixture of loving support and caution down the line. But when Charlotte arrived home sporting a neat sapphire ring on her left hand, Helen's world all but collapsed. She had to tell her then about her own involvement with the Gilmours.

Charlotte had laughed. 'How romantic, how wonderful,' then thrown her arms around Helen's neck. 'You'll be related!'

Helen had been in worse torment. Did she want to see Patrick again? Even though she had dreamt so often of a meeting. Would *he* want to see her? Could she bear the pain of her daughter married to his son, while they led separate lives?

Reclining now on the bed, Helen felt again those turbulent emotions of last year. But Charlotte had exhibited a strong determination; nothing would prevent her from becoming Mrs Daniel Gilmour. Helen picked up a small photo album; a record of Charlotte's wedding two months ago. Charlotte looked radiantly happy as Danny held onto her with tender possession. Beside Danny, in one photo, stood Patrick.

Helen's body crumpled with emotion as she looked at his dignified face. It had been inevitable that she and Patrick must meet. Charlotte had arranged a meeting for them, for lunch at a country pub, to discuss the wedding. Helen had used up every ounce of courage to get there. She wanted to make a good impression - but for whom? Her fears had turned to terror when she saw Patrick sitting alone. She had not relished meeting Patrick's wife, but it may have caused a distraction, a need for pretence.

He had smiled and reached out to touch her. Had she flinched?

'You're alone?' he frowned.

She understood his concern. 'There has only ever been Charlotte and myself.' She'd taken a deep breath. She couldn't tell him about the pain and loneliness of her life after they parted. Pain she brought on herself.

Patrick had only raised an eyebrow. His eyes had studied her face and he'd smiled again. 'I can't believe it has been so long. You've . . .'

he stopped, as uncertain as ever of committing himself to his immediate thoughts.

'Aged!' Helen volunteered. 'Twenty-four years is a long time.' She looked closely at him. His dark brown hair was evenly flecked with grey on either side of his gently matured face. He had grown from the young man who stopped hearts into the handsome man who made dreams come true.

He'd shaken his head, serious as ever. 'No. You were a pretty girl - like Charlotte.' He stopped again. But as if his thoughts had escaped any way, he added quietly, 'Will she grow into as elegant a woman as her mother?'

Helen could still feel the blush which had risen on her cheeks. To cover her feelings she'd laughingly replied, 'Does your wife let you pay compliments to other women?'

She had instantly regretted her gaucheness; the look on his face was of deep sorrow. But she was still acutely uneasy about this 'arranged' meeting.

'My wife is no longer with me. We were married fifteen years, before . . .' he made no effort to finish.

The emotions which engulfed her left her no wish to pursue it, but she *had* to ask, 'So, you did marry . . .'

'Simone!' he broke in. 'No. That would have been too cruel.'

Helen looked away so as to hide the tear that slipped unavoidably from her eye. She had fumbled for a tissue, only to be taken aback by Patrick's question.

He'd reached over and taken her hand. 'Do you forgive me, Helen?'

Her answer had been so garbled. As she now looked at the photo, she whispered, 'It was all my fault. I am so sorry Patrick.'

Tears welled up in her eyes as she sat alone in her bedroom. She wiped them away and looked at the simple cream wedding dress hanging on the wardrobe door. Tomorrow there would be different tears. *Her* daughter and *his* son would stand witness, as she became Mrs Patrick Gilmour, at last.

OH, WE DO LIKE TO BE BESIDE THE SEASIDE . . .
Matthew Jones

The Prof, daffy, bonkers, but occasionally brilliant scientist, and his faithful, cat-like robot, FE-, decided that it was time for their annual holiday.

Unfortunately, tickets for Onga Bonga Land had already been snaffled up, and the inoculations for the planet Zeutron had turned out to be too expensive. So they decided to go on holiday somewhere in the British Isles. (Anywhere abroad was out, for FE- had trouble going through the metal detectors in airports. The customs men kept taking him apart!)

In the end, after much discussion, they came up with the perfect solution. Get a map, a pin, and a blindfold.

Prof placed the map on the floor, gave FE- the pin to hold in his robot arm, and programmed him to move about randomly. Wherever the pin ended up, Prof and FE- would go. It took three tries. The duo decided that the first pin on the map would be disqualified because they didn't fancy spending two weeks in a transport cafe on the M1. The second pin ended up in Prof's leg. Eventually, they came up with Skegpool.

'Where on earth is Skegpool?' asked Prof.

'Just down the coast from Blackness!' replied FE-.

The day arrived. Prof spent ages looking for his dinosaur rubber ring, while FE- packed his bag full of nuts and bolts.

Prof programmed his travelling machine, the *Tardy,* which looks to me or you just like a large fridge. Soon it arrived. Prof looked outside. 'Do they have polar bears in Skegpool? If not, we're in the wrong place.' A few minutes later, they arrived in Skegpool.

The 5-star hotel that Prof and FE- had booked into turned out to be a rather well-worn B & B. 'Oh well, we might as well make the most of it,' moaned Prof, as images of champagne and Jacuzzis drifted from his mind.

Plucking up courage, the intrepid duo knocked timidly at the door. The door creaked open, and Big Daddy appeared. On closer inspection, it turned out to be the landlady. Before they even got over the threshold, a list of rules was thrust in front of their noses. (Well . . . Prof's nose - FE- only has a sensor.)

Rules
1 No smiling
2 No eating the parrot food
3 No smiling
4 No sandcastles in the bedroom
5 No smiling
6 No being ill on the dog
7 No smiling
8 No feeding the cat ice cream
9 Above all . . . no smiling

Prof and Fe- were directed to their room. 'Room' might be a slight stretch of the imagination. It was actually the garage, and Prof had to sleep on top of the landlady's 1987 seventh-hand Volkswagen Beetle. FE- however, was delighted, and quickly fell in love with the toolbox.

After a tour of the garage, which took a minute and a half, the duo decided to explore the local hot spots. First on their list was the amusement pier. Going into the dining room for their breakfast, Prof found two slices of toast and a note saying, *'You've missed breakfast. I'm off to the amusement pier.'*

Prof quickly snaffled the toast before FE- could lay a paw on it, and they set off to the pier.

FE- decided to try out the helter-skelter. All went well until he dropped his mat, and guess who was underneath?

'That's an improvement!' came a voice from behind the landlady, but when she turned round, shedding the coconut mat, Prof had disappeared.

As Prof rounded a corner, he saw a magnificent steam merry-go-round with rocking horses and Wurlitzer organ music. It was love at first sight!

After 26 goes without paying, Prof was finally thrown off. He meandered away towards the ice cream stall, and had all 34 flavours put in a massive cone. Unfortunately, at the moment Prof was handed the cone, FE- shot like a bullet from the end of the helter-skelter, under Prof's feet. The cone quickly obeyed the law of gravity, and plummeted onto the head of a Big Daddy-esque figure in the queue behind.

Totally oblivious to the chaos surrounding them, Prof and FE- went over to a sweet stall and bought some sticks of rock with 'LoopgekS ot emocleW' through the middle to send home as presents. Then Prof rode the scariest ride in the whole place.

'What do we do now?' asked Prof, still shaky at the knees after the galloping ponies.

'Aren't we supposed to wear funny hats? Like that holidaymaker in Crocodile Dundee did . . . you know . . . big, floppy hat, with corks hanging down . . .' replied FE-.

'That's in Australia, you fool, and we don't happen to be in the southern hemisphere. But you have given me an idea . . .'

Prof dragged a reluctant FE- towards he seafront, where there are a number of shops boasting sales of *'Head Gear!'* The choice was staggering. FE-, being rather naive about hats, chose a Tesco bag from the floor of the shop, and tried to fit it round his sensors.

Prof, meanwhile, was trying on hats with messages. After several kisses on the cheek from various people, Prof decided to buy a fake pirate hat, complete with stuffed shoulder parrot. Feeling like typical holidaymakers, the two discovered a small cinema. Unfortunately, the cashier told Prof that all the extreme video nasties like 'Revenge Of The Mutant Splat Gore Monster' and 'The Sludge Creature Meets Vermin Man' had sold out, and the only film showing was 'Bambi Meets Peter Pan'. Unsurprisingly, neither Prof or FE- wanted to watch this.

'What now?' asked Prof.

'Well,' said FE-, 'there's a Junch and Pudy stand down at the seafront.' (FE- mixed up his words due to his Tesco bag interfering with his sensors.)

FE- and Prof sat down before the show. At first, they didn't know why the characters were slurring their words. Prof then realised that the Punch and Judy man was drunk. This was confirmed when Mr Punch started singing rude words to the tune of 'Jerusalem'. Prof and FE- decided to do something, being worried about the kiddies. They crept round the back of the stall, and tried to hijack the show. Unfortunately, the Punch and Judy man fought back. The whole farrago ended with the stall collapsing. Mr Punch reappeared, singing 'Jerusalem' triumphantly.

Prof and FE- realised that they were probably in trouble with the landlady, so they snuck back to the *Tardy*. (Also, Prof didn't want to pay the bill.) Prof programmed the *Tardy* to leave on Friday, 13th of

July at 13.13 exactly. Fe-'s query as to whether that was a bit unlucky was overruled by Prof.

He thought differently when they got home, as FE- had left the taps on, the garden was a lake, and as Prof opened the door, a huge wave of water rolled over him.

FIRE FROM HELL
(Dedicated to Sally Adams)
Gerard Allardyce

Uncle Reg served in the London Fire Brigade for fifty years. He joined as a boy of fifteen until he retired at the age of sixty-five in 1974.

The years before the Second World War were halcyon days for him in the London Fire Brigade. He purchased a launch on the Thames. Then he courted a young lady called Eileen who was later to become my auntie.

'I have brought back peace in our time,' Neville Chamberlain claimed as he came back from Munich, but soon there was to be a terrible war which would test the likes of Uncle Reg and his friends to the limits of their endurance.

In 1940, the German Luftwaffe were bombing London and that city was soon set alight. The London Fire Brigade was soon using horse-drawn vehicles as there was a shortage of motorised fire engines. If 1940 was a dreadful year for Uncle Reg, 1941 was even worse. Fires were even worse as the bombing intensified. In the meantime, Uncle Reg's launch was requisitioned for fire fighting from the river by the fire brigade.

'Nothing was worse than that episode,' Uncle Reg reflected later. A large warehouse was burning by the river in the docklands. A Team was ordered into the warehouse to put the fire out. Uncle Reg was in A Team and A Team went into the burning warehouse. Uncle Reg reflected afterwards, if the burning timbers didn't kill his colleagues, then the rats did, who gouged out the throats of the firemen. Uncle Reg was the only fireman to come out of the burning building unscathed. The station commander then ordered B Team to go in, with the same result. All of them were killed by rats or by falling debris. Uncle Reg was burnt on his back. He was then taken to hospital after being called to that fire.

Auntie Eileen visited Uncle Reg in hospital where he was being treated for burns on his back, as well as suffering from a complete nervous breakdown. He was in hospital for only three weeks. The resolve for fighting the fires where so many of his friends had died was uppermost in his mind.

'What are you thinking about Reg?'

'I'm going back to the fire brigade to be with my friends. Here in London, my love, it's been like the fire from Hell.' He smiled bravely from his hospital bed, whilst outside the bells of an ambulance could be heard in the distance approaching the hospital.

THE LITTLE JAVA MOUSE
Mo Ross

Luke awoke with a start, wondering where he was. He could hear sounds coming from the room and he looked around and then remembered where he was, in England.

Grandma Travanna was busy in the kitchen making breakfast, it had taken a long time to get here, he was still a little tired.

'Hello dear, time to get up and have some nice breakfast, we have a busy day ahead of us. I must show you around.' Grandma Travanna was looking at him with her big brown eyes and she had a big hairy chin. Her whiskers were grey now, but in times gone by she had been a very beautiful lady mouse. All the men said she was lovely. Grandma Travanna had chosen Luke's Grandad Frederick to be her man and they had lived in the Big House ever since. Grandad was asleep; he'd had a busy night trying to find things to eat.

'Today we are going to see Aunt Bea in the attic. It's a long journey and a bit dangerous, so you will have to stay close to me,' Grandma said.

'The house was big, I came to this room through a lot of tunnels and very dusty passages,' Grandad said, awake now after his nap. 'I had to be very quiet because of the cat.'

Luke had not seen the cat yet, but they were not very big in India, and also very lazy out there.

'Come on, put your coat on and wrap up warm, then we will be off,' Grandma said.

She went to go out of the front door, but suddenly there was a loud sound, like a fire engine, and she shot back in. 'Phew, that was close,' Grandma said, shaking all over and very white.

'What's the matter?' Luke asked, very worried indeed.

'That was the cat,' she said. 'We will have to wait for a little while, it's very dangerous at the moment.'

Luke didn't get a good look at the cat as Grandma had pulled him back too soon. It sounded very big.

Grandad had woken up with all the noise and jumped up and gave Grandma a cuddle, as she slowly got over the shock of seeing the cat. 'Never mind, try again in a little while,' he said. 'He can't stay there forever, he will get hungry soon anyway.'

They all had a cup of rose tea and listened to the radio for a bit.

'Try again now,' Grandad said. 'Aunt Bea will be wondering where you have got to.'

They all stepped very quietly out into the room. It was very bright and huge, and was the biggest room Luke had ever seen. The lights were very bright in the ceiling and made his eyes go funny; they looked like the sun in India. Grandma was running now and Luke had to jump to keep up with her. There was a long table in the room and they all hid behind the legs to take a break.

'We have to go up the back way to the attic, it's too dangerous to take the stairs,' whispered Grandma.

There were heavy footsteps coming their way, it was the lord of the house. He was big and heavy with a big, red face. He was shouting to his footman to get his horse ready and had what seemed to be a large coloured glass in his hand. He was dressed in a bright blue riding suit and had a funny-shaped hat on his head. The two mice kept very still and quiet, just like Luke did back in India when any of the humans were around. The lord carried on down the hall still shouting and making a lot of noise, his footman following on behind.

'Come on, let's go!' Grandma said.

They all walked to the back of the house and up the narrow, dark stairs to the attic. Aunt Bea was there to greet them and threw her arms around Luke. She gave him a big hug, nearly knocking off his turban.

'My, what a handsome boy you are, so smart in your suit. Did you have a good journey over from India?' she asked.

'Yes thank you, Aunt Bea, but it was a long way and I'm a bit tired today.'

'Never mind, come and meet Joe,' she said.

In the corner of the room sat a very small mouse with green eyes and a shiny black coat. He looked at Luke for a few minutes before he spoke. 'What's your name?' he asked.

'Luke,' was the reply.

'Come and see my fish,' he said.

'Don't be too long and try to stay clean,' Aunt Bea said as they left the room.

Through an alleyway at the back of the room there was a little hollow in the woodwork.

'Just through here,' said Joe as he called Luke over.

He climbed up and through the hollow; it was very small, inside there was a glass bowl with a tiny orange fish swimming around in it.

'What do you think?' Joe asked.

Luke had seen fish twice as big in India, but didn't want to hurt his feelings, so he said, 'I think it's great.'

Joe smiled, feeling very proud of his little fish and himself.

'Joe! Luke!' Aunt Bea called out

They both clambered back out of the hollow and into the room, both of them looking a bit dusty.

'Oh dear me, just look at you two,' Aunt Bea said, hurriedly dusting them down. 'What a mess you're in.'

The table was set for dinner and Luke was very hungry. Over dinner, Grandma told Aunt Bea about the cat, but Luke couldn't see what all the fuss was about, it sounded big, but he wasn't sure how big.

'Have you seen the cat?' Luke asked Joe.

Joe's green eyes became very big and scared looking. 'Oh yes,' he said, nearly choking on one of his potatoes.

'Quiet, you two!' Grandma said.

Both of them stopped talking straight away. Luke felt bad for forgetting his manners at the dinner table and continued to eat, in silence of course.

'I will bring Joe down tomorrow so you two can play again,' said Aunt Bea.

They finished dinner afterwards and got ready to leave.

'Be careful and try not to worry,' Aunt Bea said.

Grandma looked tired but managed to give her a reassuring smile as she left.

On the way home Grandma was very quiet and so was the house, it was quite spooky. The doors looked bigger in the dark, a lot bigger and scary. Human voices and strange noises came from some of the rooms and from other dark corners of the big house. The floors had lovely thick carpets on them, each one a different colour. Their fluffy texture kept tickling Luke's toes, but thankfully, no sign of the cat.

When they got home, Grandad was sitting reading a great big book by the fire. As Grandma and Luke came in, he got up from his chair and came over and gave them both a hug, very pleased that they were back safely.

Luke set off to bed feeling very tired after his busy day and so did Grandma and Grandad. They were all dreaming about their day except for his grandma who hoped she wouldn't dream at all about the cat.

Aunt Bea and Joe arrived early the next morning. Grandma was very pleased to see them and a lot happier today.

'Can we go outside and explore?' Joe shouted excitedly.

Aunt Bea's face went all serious looking. 'I don't know, Luke is new around here, it could be dangerous.'

'Please, please!' Joe pleaded, his green eyes falsely moistening a little.

'OK but be careful of the cat,' she said.

Joe and Luke went a back way through some tunnels and came out into the kitchen.

'This is where we can get some cheese,' Joe whispered.

It was very noisy, humans bustling around cooking and chattering away. Joe and Luke went to the side of the table. Joe looked over at the fridge.

'In there,' he said.

Suddenly a great big shadow fell across them and a great big hairy face with wide eyes was just crouching, looking at them.

'Quick, run,' Joe screamed.

They ran and the cat chased after them, but Joe fell over. Luke helped him up, his heart pounding. The cat was big and making that awful fire engine sound he had heard the day before with his grandma. Joe threw himself down a hole in the floor and Luke followed.

Safe at last, they were very relieved to be alive. They must have fallen through a small ceiling as there was lots of dust and dirt around, most of it over them.

'Who's making all this mess?' a voice growled.

A funny little mouse in a tartan shirt with long hair and a beard was looking down on them.

'I'm hurt,' Joe said, crying a little.

'Let's have a look at you. My name's Angus,' the mouse said.

'The leg's not too bad, let's get a bandage on it. Where did you come from?' he asked.

'The kitchen,' Luke said. 'The cat was chasing us.'

'My, my, you were lucky then. What's your name?' he asked.

'My name's Luke and this is Joe.'

'Where do you come from? I haven't seen you around here before,' the long-haired mouse asked.

'I'm on holiday from India,' Luke said shyly.

'No, no, I meant where do you come from in the house?' the mouse chortled.

'I don't know, I have only been here for a couple of days,' Luke answered sheepishly, 'but Joe lives in the attic.' He was trying to sound a bit bolder than before.

'The attic, that's a long way,' said Angus.

Joe had become quite sleepy now, so Angus put him on his bed. 'Must be the excitement. Oh well, you won't be going anywhere for a little while, let's have some tea.'

Luke drank his tea, but it did not taste as nice as Grandma's tea, he didn't say anything though, but remembered his manners. His grandma would have been pleased with him; he could behave when he wanted to.

'Where am I?' Luke asked, looking around and spotting a curious looking object on the floor.

'In the basement at the bottom of the house,' Angus answered. 'It's a long way back to the attic. Don't worry though, I'll get you home.' *Wherever home is*, Angus thought.

'I think I live somewhere in between if you know what I mean,' Luke said.

'We will ask Joe when he wakes up, he'll know,' said Angus.

Luke stared at this thing on the floor. It looked like a funny bag with pipes and Luke had never seen anything like it before, ever. Angus turned around and saw Luke, his eyes staring at the floor; suddenly he let out a great big laugh which made Luke jump.

'Oh you've seen it then, they are called bagpipes and they make a noise,' Angus said as he picked them up.

Luke looked scared. Angus saw this in his eyes and laughed again.

'There is nothing to be afraid of, you have to blow in this pipe and squeeze this bag. It makes music,' Angus explained. 'I use it to scare the cat, it works very well.' Angus blew on the bagpipes. Suddenly a high-pitched sound filled the room, and Luke covered over his ears.

'What is that awful noise?' asked a little voice coming from the bedroom. 'Is the cat back again?' Joe was awake at last.

'No, they're bagpipes,' Angus said.

'What?' asked Joe.

'Don't worry, I'll explain,' said Luke and so he did, glad that Joe was finally awake and could tell Angus where he lived.

Luke and Joe had no idea how to get back but Angus knew the house well. He knew how to get them back home safely through the service elevators which ran from floor to floor throughout the house as he had used them before.

THE UNEXPLAINED JOURNEY
Susie Field

'Dust to dust, ashes to ashes.'

The words were spoken quietly as Bob threw a single rose onto Maggie's coffin. He gazed around the small churchyard - so many sad faces. Maggie's twin sons from her first marriage - their wives and children weeping softly, and of course Ellie, their beautiful daughter, heavy with child and grasping her husband's arm as the tears flowed unchecked.

'Are you okay, Daddy?' Ellie asked, moving towards her father.

Bob forced a smile as the unbearable heartache ripped through his body. 'I was lost in thought, Ellie,' he whispered. 'I should be thankful for the 28 years of marriage I had with your mother. It wasn't always easy. I remember when we first met. I was ten years younger than your mum and she was divorced. The twins were in their teens. They objected to me at first but I never gave up on them - we became friends eventually.'

Ellie stole a glance at her father. He had just turned 60 - it had been a quiet celebration - just close family. Maggie had insisted - said it was important, but she had looked so ill as the cancer travelled through her body and a week later she had passed away in his arms. He had always been a tall, handsome man and it troubled her to see him now, broken and fragile.

'It's time to go,' Ellie said softly.

He took her hand and climbed into the waiting car. Ellie had prepared a small buffet and drinks were available. Friends were telling him how sorry they were, that it would feel better in time. He answered them all politely - yet his voice sounded strange to his own ears, distant and unfamiliar. He was glad when it was over - would it ever be really over?

The following week was not easy for Bob. Family and friends rallied round but all he wanted was Maggie back in his life. He grabbed his coat and headed for the cemetery, telling himself he needed the exercise - but all he needed was to be with Maggie.

He sat quietly near her grave, as sorrow and despair engulfed him. It was raining heavily and he didn't want to leave her alone. Glancing at his watch, he reluctantly headed for the gates. Ellie always telephoned at 6.30 and he didn't want her to worry - especially in her condition. *Maggie would have loved another grandchild*, he thought, bending his head as the weather deteriorated. The rain was lashing against his face as he hurried home. He remembered the screech of brakes as he stepped into the road and the bright lights of the lorry as it hurtled towards him. People were screaming, loud anxious voices, then nothing - just an empty blackness.

Ellie was sobbing at her father's bedside. 'Please don't die, Daddy,' she begged.

The doctor had said he was in a coma and although his physical injuries were not serious, the blow to his head was causing them concern. They told her he'd stepped out directly into the path of an oncoming lorry. Surely it hadn't been deliberate - her father would never do that. Yet he was so sick with grief, maybe he wanted to die.

Bob could feel himself moving upwards away from the empty blackness, a terrible force gripping his whole body, yet there was no pain. He felt to be at peace as he floated towards the light. He could hear laughter, chattering voices. He wasn't alone. Happy faces beckoned him forward and he was laughing with them, it was a beautiful place. He hadn't laughed for a long time. It felt good. He was now hurtling towards the light, it was blinding as he drifted helplessly forward.

'Bob. What are you doing here?' It was Maggie, he could see her, she was with him. There was no pain on her face, she was young and beautiful. She held out her hand and then she stopped and moved away from him. 'You must go back,' she said.

He didn't want to - he wanted to stay.

'I'm all right my darling,' her voice floated towards him as she pushed him into the blackness.

'No. Maggie, please,' he begged.

'It isn't your time,' she said gently. She was slipping away towards the light. 'I will always love you Bob, but I'm happy now. I'm at peace here, there is no pain. Ellie needs you. We will meet again - but not yet.'

He was falling - Maggie was waving as her final words caressed him.

'I love you. I miss you so much, but please go back, your life is not over. Be happy for me. I don't want you to be sad.'

The force was pulling him back into the black abyss.

He could hear voices again - then a gentle voice, like Maggie's - it was Ellie.

'Oh, thank God,' Ellie said.

He slowly opened his eyes. He was surrounded, doctors, nurses and Ellie, smiling down at him, the mirror image of Maggie.

'Daddy, I thought we'd lost you as well,' she sobbed.

'I've been with Maggie,' he replied softly.

Ellie looked startled. 'What do you mean? Have you been dreaming?'

'I don't know sweetheart. Maybe I have. Yet I saw her and she spoke to me.'

'Would you like to tell me about it?' Ellie asked.

'I was lost in a strange blackness - I don't know for how long,' Bob replied.

'Four weeks,' Ellie explained. 'You've been in a coma for four weeks. There was an accident. They said you stepped out into the path of a lorry. Was it an accident, Daddy?' She had to know. Relief swept through her as he nodded.

'Yes it was. I had been to the cemetery. It was raining heavily and I was thinking about Maggie. I didn't see the lorry, just heard the brakes and then nothing.'

'What happened next?' Ellie questioned. She was intrigued.

'I was lifted out of the blackness. It's hard to explain, it was so real. People were happy and laughing. I wanted to go with them towards the light, it was pulling me forward - then I heard Maggie. She was smiling at me and talking in that gentle, familiar voice. She looked young again, no longer in pain. She said she missed me and loved me, but it wasn't my time. She pushed me back and I tried to stay. I didn't want to lose her again, but she said we would be together one day - but not yet. She sent me back, Ellie. She said you needed me.'

'I do,' Ellie sobbed.

'I bet you think I'm crazy don't you?' he laughed.

It was good to see him laugh again.

'No, I don't,' Ellie replied thoughtfully. 'Something must have happened. Who knows, maybe it was a dream - but I'm glad Mummy sent you back to me.' She leaned over and kissed his cheek and then he noticed.

'You had the baby?' he asked.

'Yes I did,' she smiled. 'A little girl.'

'I'm a grandad!' Bob exclaimed. 'Is she alright? Are you okay darling?' He was suddenly anxious. He had missed so much in such a short time. Life was precious, he wanted to live it again.

'We're both fine,' Ellie grinned. 'Colin's in the waiting room with the baby.'

He watched her leave. Slim and dark - just like Maggie. 'Oh she is so beautiful.' Bob felt the tears prick his eyes as Ellie placed the tiny child in his arms. 'Maggie would have loved her, Ellie.'

'I know she would,' she replied sadly. 'We must carry her in our hearts now.'

'What's her name?' Bob asked as the small baby clamped her little gums around his finger.

'Her name's Maggie,' Ellie replied quietly.

Bob took her hand and squeezed it gently, unable to speak - the tears rolling down his pale cheeks, but he looked at peace.

Bob spent the following six weeks in hospital and then returned home. The house was quiet without Maggie, and he still missed her - but it was easier as time moved on. The pain of losing her was always with him, although it didn't hurt quite so much.

He was standing at the school gates waiting for Maggie.

'Hello again.' The voice was familiar.

'Hello Sandra,' he replied pleasantly.

They had chatted many times before - her grandson was in the same class as Maggie. She was a good looking woman, probably in her mid-fifties and he knew she was a widow from their previous conversations. Sandra was always smartly dressed, her short salt and pepper hair carefully styled.

'It's a beautiful day,' she continued.

He nodded in reply. The conversation flowed easily. Bob enjoyed talking to her. He loved his family but over the last few months he had missed female company.

'I was wondering,' Sandra hesitated. 'I've been given two complimentary theatre tickets for Saturday night. Would you like to join me?'

He looked astonished - she was asking him on a date.

'It's a pity to waste them. You'll be quite safe. I promise to behave myself,' she laughed.

'I'd love to, thank you,' Bob replied, joining in her laughter. 'We could go for a meal afterwards. My treat.'

'You're on,' she answered, scribbling down her address. 'About seven. Is that okay?'

He nodded and found he was looking forward to it.

'Grandad.' Little Maggie ran towards him, her black curls dancing.

'How was school?' he asked, swinging her around.

'It was okay,' she squealed. 'Are we going to put flowers on Gran's grave?'

He nodded. He still went every week but never alone - Ellie wouldn't allow it. He smiled down at little Maggie as she carefully arranged the flowers - standing back to admire her work.

'Do you miss her a lot?' She always noticed the sadness in his eyes.

'Very much,' he replied, taking her small hand in his own. 'I went to see her once.'

'Really? How come?' Maggie asked - she didn't really understand and he didn't want to frighten her. He thought carefully before replying. 'Before you were born darling. I had an accident. I crossed the road without looking both ways.'

'That was naughty,' Maggie replied simply.

'Yes it was. You must never do that. Anyway, I was very hurt and I nearly died. I was travelling to Heaven and then your gran sent me back.'

'Was she sad?' Maggie asked.

'No, she was happy. She was very ill before she died. It was time for her to leave us.'

'Was it a dream?' Maggie thought it was all rather confusing.

'I'm not sure love - maybe. Some things cannot be explained.'

Maggie nodded solemnly.

'Why don't we take a walk in the park?' he said suddenly - desperate to change the subject. 'We could feed the ducks.'

Maggie squealed with delight as they hurried on their way. 'I'm glad she sent you back, Grandad.'

He squeezed her small hand. 'So am I sweetheart. So am I.'

Bob's friendship with Sandra blossomed. She was a good companion and they enjoyed the simple pleasures of life - trips to the theatre - quiet dinners - even the odd weekend away. Bob was thankful for the extra time spent with Sandra and their families.

Several years later, after a short illness and surrounded by loved ones - Bob passed away. He travelled again through the empty blackness, but he was no longer afraid.

'I've been waiting for you my darling,' Maggie beckoned in the gentle voice he remembered so well. She took his hand and they were laughing together as they headed towards the light.

HIS CALLING
Gloria Hargreaves

She went into hospital with wind and came out with Thomas. This set the pattern of their lives for many moons to come. Paddy, his father, had moaned, 'You take too much bicarb'. It made her belch loudly and frequently. Now he had something else to complain about, not that he was there too often. The pub down the road had a very loud call.

Howth was a delightful little fishing village just outside the city of Dublin. Their little well-kept cottage nestled under the hill close to the harbour. Every curtain and carpet exuded the smell of fish. Not that anybody minded, this was what they had known for all of their lives and they were proud of their surroundings.

Thomas spent the first five years of his life bawling or balancing precariously on the harbour wall. Paddy spent more and more time in the local. Mam spent more and more of her time praying to the Lord or saying her beads. 'God preserve me, that child will be the death of me, he puts the heart across me.' She supped the odd Guinness for strength. 'How was I to know that six Guinnesses later, after Benediction on a Sunday afternoon, Thomas would be the result?'

She remembered that Dr O'Grady had told her she was barren and Paddy always said she was frigid - sure she'd believed them, something had gone badly wrong somewhere. She recalled how Sister Mary Michael had told the whole class, 'Evil thoughts and open legs lead to ruination'. Is this what she had meant?

As time went by, she began to enjoy more and more being with her young son. His shock of red hair and freckles on his nose reminded her of her kindly father. She would recount with regret how sleep depravation had filled her with thankless words. And Paddy's behaviour under the sheets gave her little more pleasure than a quick hiccup.

Thomas didn't excel at anything. His reports read 'doesn't apply himself'; 'we wonder why he bothers to attend'; 'lives in his own world', but she didn't mind too much.

He was a good lad and his father barely noticed either of them. Uncurling Thomas' wire spectacles occupied a major part of each evening. That was when he hadn't mislaid or lost them. 'Fell down a manhole' one of his milder excuses as Mam scraped together the pennies to get him yet another pair.

Many a candle was lit or a novena prayed on her Rosary for an improvement in his eyesight. 'Not a family thing, we can all see in the dark' she was heard to mutter. 'Sure he'd slip over an idea if he had one'!

Thomas' idea of bliss was to wait for hours 'til the fishing boats came into harbour in the late afternoon. Mam would often come down and wrap a coat around his shoulders to protect him from the elements.

'You'll catch your death.'

He took no notice. He'd help the weary fishermen sort their catch, unravel their nets and hose down their deck. He felt important here and was often rewarded with three fat herrings for their Friday supper.

'Sure, you're a grand kid, don't know what I'd do without you' made him feel good. Woe betide meat should cross their lips on a Friday.

'Devil's work chewing hard on a Friday,' Mam said.

Wonder if that's why Gran had false teeth? No jeering from his schoolmates here, no 'specky four-eyes' nor 'you ginger eejit'. No teasing because he wouldn't join in their street games or play football. Who wants to hop on one leg? No, he was important here. They couldn't leap as he could onto a slippery deck without losing his footing; they couldn't swirl the hose into every nook and cranny on the deck. This was his domain and these were his friends.

When his twelfth birthday arrived, old Sean rewarded him by taking him out for a catch for the very first time.

He was so excited he couldn't get to sleep that night, despite his mother's promise to awaken him at 3am. He lay on his bed fully dressed, complete with woollen socks, heavy top coat, all ready for the off.

Bleary-eyed he dashed to the harbour arriving pink-cheeked and breathless, ready for the greatest adventure of his young life. He had only one regret, the school bullies could not see him, how jealous they would be. With spray in his face and wind in his hair, he sat to share his sardine sandwiches with old Sean. The smell of his favourite lunch indistinguishable from the smells around him. Mam had made them especially for his birthday lunch and he felt overwhelming joy at this glorious experience. With pride in his heart he pulled and tugged on the nets 'til his palms bled. One word of praise from old Sean spurring him to greater effort.

'You have it in your blood lad, you'll make a fine fisherman one day.'

Arriving home late in the afternoon, exhausted but elated, he fell into a fitful sleep with a clear picture in his mind of what he wanted to be one day.

His father died when he was little past sixteen and he took his place as head of the household.

'Trust him to rot his liver and desert us,' Mam said.

Father Walsh prayed for him to enter the Pearly Gates and said what a loving husband and father he'd been. Don't think he knew what he was talking about. Wonder if there's a pub behind the Pearly Gates?

Income was now needed. Thomas' pay was meagre but his title bold. 'Apprentice fisherman'. Working all hours didn't bother him one bit, despite the rain, sleet and snow. He toiled hard and purposefully, dreaming of the day he would have his own boat. He was determined to learn everything he could. Sunrise elated him, the glow invigorated his senses. He was poetic and would throw words to the wind. 'Fish wait for me, I'm halfway across the sea. When I fling my nets be there. There's a pact between God and me. We, the lovers of the sea'. Sometimes his fellow fishermen would smile and call him a daft bugger; other times they'd exclaim, 'Ah sure, you're a man of many words'. Whatever, he was happy. This was the nearest place to Heaven.

When the years passed and he reached his 21st birthday, he knew he had reached his big day. Gran had promised to help him get his very own boat. A pretty grotty affair, in need of paint, elbow-grease and tender love and affection. There was plenty of that around. He slaved and made it sea-worthy.

Mam sat on the harbour wall with a tear in her eye, as he set out on his very first trip in charge. He felt buoyant, alert and total man.

Mam waved and shouted, 'Goodbye. God love you, me son. Go pull them in.' She thought of his arrival, how difficult life had been at times, but how worthwhile it all had been.

'The Call Of The Wind' rode the waves well.

SOUVENIR
M C Jones

London Waterloo was packed on Saturday morning, with all its trains and passengers ready to go. Nice and early, people had arrived with their families and their belongings in a jumble of luggage and language, in anticipation of a long journey. This particular station included the Eurostar terminal, the rail link with Paris.

Up the escalator, into the departure lounge, tickets and passports at the ready, people waited to board the train, quite excitedly. They stood in the bars and cafes and browsed the shops, killing time whilst preparations were made.

'Passengers for the 12.05 Eurostar to Paris, Gare du Nord, should now make their way to gate number . . .'

The announcement crackled all over the station as travellers reached for their documentation. Once through all the security checks, they headed down the steps and onto the platform. There, gleaming at a standstill, was the Eurostar.

Passengers filed on board to their respective seats, and bags were stowed away, above and behind. The swish interiors of the train were suddenly full of people talking animatedly, their smiles and gestures reflected in the windows. There were tourists chattering, businessmen talking and youngsters laughing in their places. And in carriage 4, seat 18, there was Turner.

He'd had a brainstorm one day and decided it was time for a few days off. He was travelling alone to Paris for the weekend. Turner was an unremarkable man, pale and quietly-spoken and unused to all this. He was of medium height, looks and character, and kept himself to himself.

After a further delay, some anxious moments and a few announcements, their journey began: Eurostar rolled forwards.

Slowly at first, the train emerged from beneath the glass roof of Waterloo station, and began to gather speed. The windows filled with the suburbs of the capital and the skyline which fell away as they headed south into the countryside. In the afternoon light the towns and cities and the counties in which they were set seemed quaintly asleep next to this massive engineering achievement.

The picture postcard villages stirred as the train passed through on its way to the coast. The view out of the window changed from farmland and commuter belt to oast houses and orchards, and then the approach to the 'chunnel' was announced over the speakers.

Their departure from the UK was unexpected and something of an anticlimax. The huge concrete entrance to the channel tunnel was a long way from the coast at Dover. The passengers were taken by surprise as the windows went dark and the interior lighting of the carriages took over. Turner had always been apprehensive about this part of the journey. It was 20 minutes in transit, Dover to Calais, and the pressure on his eardrums was becoming more and more intense.

The talk became very hushed and people huddled together in their seats, some with concern written all over their faces. As the train progressed through the channel tunnel, it was difficult to believe they were travelling along the sea bed.

Finally, Eurostar burst out of the tunnel and into the sunlight. Suddenly there was northern France all around them. It was as if they had awoken from a bad dream. Turner shook himself and sat up in seat 18 to see the beauty of the French afternoon as they slowed into Calais station. After picking up a token number of passengers, the driver set off again, having announced the one hour time difference and their estimated time of arrival in Paris. This time, he was free of the speed limits imposed in the UK and accelerated fast. Soon they were rushing along at over a hundred miles per hour.

Turner took note of his surroundings as the train raced through the rural areas. Farms and hamlets lay in the heat, the land bronze and gold in the lateness of the day. They swept through towns and villages unspoilt and silent in the country. He noticed that the weather improved as they moved south and temperatures rose as they approached the capital. Soon they were approaching the environs of the capital, slowing down gradually and steadily until the train came to a halt at the Gare du Nord. Passengers alighted here and Turner plus luggage walked down the platform, through the station itself and out into the open air. He called a taxi and crossed the city, lively with traffic, to the Avenue Bosquet and the Prince Hotel.

His room was small and sparsely furnished and opened out onto the backyard of the hotel. There was no view to speak of save that of the dustbins and the other rooms which rose a couple of floors over his head.

The following morning after a breakfast of croissants and café au lait, Turner set out on foot through the capital. He'd seen a sign on the way in for the Eiffel Tower and made off in that direction.

Crossing the road and threading his way through all the pedestrians, he turned right into the Champs de Mar, the park surrounding the tower. Beyond the trees, the fountains, the gracious lawns and pathways, there was France's most famous landmark, rising hundreds of feet into the air.

'Excusez-moi, monsieur,' said a voice behind him.

He turned around quickly. There was an American-accented female, medium height and blonde with a smile. She rearranged herself and her male companion to stand in front of the tower and handed the camera to Turner.

'Would you take our picture for us please?' she asked sweetly.

'Of course . . .' he replied, clearing his throat and coughing. He found their image in the lens and pressed the shutter, then handed the camera back to the happy couple.

'Thank you,' they said, before linking arms and strolling off through the trees.

'My pleasure,' Turner replied as he watched them go.

He spent the whole day in the area around the tower, mingling with the crowds and falling for the girls. Later, as the day matured, evening filled the park and the breeze which blew overhead had Air France written all over it. He returned to his hotel and relaxed in front of some rather strange television programmes, falling asleep for a while in the process. After changing his shirt and washing in the hand basin, he went next door to 'Vingt sur Vin', the little café that served tourists with meals and snacks. Turner strung together a few sentences in French, and thought deeply as he ordered steak, fries and a cola.

And so it went on for the next 48 hours. He became a sightseer, crossing the city by metro, visiting the boutiques and street cafés, basking in sunshine like orangina. The Champs Elysees, the Arc de Triomphe, the gendarmes and the musea, the river, the boats and the tourists. He was overwhelmed by it all.

Threading his way through the Citroens and the Renaults, he explored the unspoilt tree-lined avenues and the beautiful boulevards of the capital. He wandered nonchalantly through the Latin quarter, took a train to the Porte d'Orleans. He went over the bridge to the Ile de France and left euros and cents in the collecting box at Notre Dame. He watched the TGV heading south, and dined in the brasseries and bistros on the left bank of the Seine.

Just before leaving, Turner felt drawn to Les Invalides and the golden dome that reigned over this part of Paris. Inexplicably he found himself ascending the steps, first to the church and then to the adjacent museum. Catholicism and all its accompanying ceremony came crashing into his spirit, especially on seeing the statue of Christ and the massive crucifix hanging by one of the altars.

And then, the reason for his visit. Beneath the giant dome lay the tomb of Napoleon Bonaparte. Turner approached slowly, passed all the paintings on the walls, the various statues and mementoes of the man's life. There was a collection of furniture, uniforms, objets d'art, many of them acquired during the military campaigns of the 1800s. Turner saw it all until eventually his eyes came to rest on the throne. An extravagant issue, ornate and covered in gold leaf, with a purple seat. The letter N was embroidered into the velvet.

The tomb itself consisted of a monstrous wooden carving which seemed to say something of the notoriety achieved by the man in his lifetime. Turner was struck by the nonsense and the infamy of the man whose remains lay within the tomb. He fled the scene, hurrying to the Gare du Nord and the return journey.

Many years later, he was at home in England. Grey-haired and a little overweight, thoughtful and with a tendency to reminisce. He had a modest home, the result of a chequered career and full of things that were not worth very much to anyone except himself. He had mementoes from a generation ago - a likeness of Gustav Eiffel, for instance, purchased in a boutique in Paris. It was enough to remind him of his trip to France. 'Je me souviens' said the souvenir in his living room at home. The memories came flooding back every time he looked upon it.

And of course, he went back on Eurostar more than once. All the way back - Prince Hotel, Avenue Bosquet, and so on and so forth. Out of season, he took his walks and had his meals and joined the people in the park.

By an act of God, he was one day stopped by a couple in late middle age with their three teenage kids. Everything about them was from the United States. They were a charming family and Turner spoke with them very briefly. It was wonderful to hear those American voices. He had always wanted to visit the USA but had never managed to do so. Not for the first time, they handed him a camera and asked him to oblige.

'Turn the camera,' asked one of the daughters.

He turned it ninety degrees and pressed the shutter, capturing the parents and the children in one sublime irony in front of the tower.

Sometimes his travels become too much for him. Sometimes his emotions were overcome. On this final journey, things were even more lyrical and poignant than ever. SNCF, autumn leaves, children in the streets - September in Paris, seen through the eyes of an Englishman who lived in the past.

And times have changed: the modern world carried on growing and mutating in a continuum of science and cynicism. Skyscrapers rose and fell, there were births and deaths ad infinitum. It has been happening all his life and Turner saw nothing in it to write home about.

Elsewhere, N stirred in his grave at Les Invalides, restless at the thought of it all.

MY NAME IS . . .
G K (Bill) Baker

It seems but five minutes since I was playing in the dusty earth outside my father's hut, but even then my games were always on the warlike side. I usually finished up dreaming of owning a modern rifle . . . not just a weapon that had long been consigned to the scrapheap and then resurrected by some member of my tribe, but a brand new weapon that any modern lad such as myself could be proud of.

But such dreams, alas, were most unlikely to be realised (if at all) until I grew up, so I contented myself by becoming the leader of a gang of boys of my own age, armed with sticks and knives with which we terrorised the weaker members of our community. It was this type of upbringing that was ideal for the terrorist that I was to become.

And so it was that I grew into my evil ways, brushing aside all signs of weakness amongst my fellow tribesmen, and constantly hatching new ideas to torment the rest of the world which had now become my sworn enemy.

I soon found out that I could do little on my own, so I became a teacher, not of ABCs but of how to make bombs, and soon became proficient in this type of terrorism. I found out that gelignite was not only the best for the job but was the most easy explosive to obtain when one had a band of terrorists such as I had to steal whatever they wanted.

Unfortunately, it seemed only too soon that my name became a household word, and it became necessary for me to go into hiding to carry out the various plots I had made, plots that would shake the world.

It was about that time that my life changed, and all because of a Baptist priest that my men had captured with a view to getting some ransom. That Baptist priest had the oiliest tongue I had ever come across, and in no time at all had me wondering if the path I had chosen was the right path. He had no fear at all of me or my men, in fact, he had no fear of anything, saying that his God (which was the same God which we called Allah) would protect him always as long as he believed in Him.

I listened to all he had to say, and the more I listened, the more I came to realise that there was a great deal of truth in what he said. I tried to catch him out, but he had an answer to everything I put to him. I couldn't believe that any man could have such faith, especially as he was so close to death by the ruffians that had captured him.

And then it happened! I found that I believed him. Everything that he had said made sense. What was I to do? I couldn't carry on being a terrorist. I had to do something to let the world know that I was no longer a threat to them. I put it to the Baptist priest who had an answer to everything.

His answer was, 'Come with me and confess your sins, and God will take care of you. There is your answer, Osama bin Laden!'

WHEN WE WERE TOUGH
Stephen Humphries

The drive down to his parents' place always made him anxious, even now. Thomas drove his Ford Mondeo with the sales rep's mileage through the evening traffic, thankful for once for the rush hour, he was in no hurry to arrive. He made the trip every second week and his wife thought he was crazy. She might have had a point. Thomas' parents were lucky if they saw her once a year. She usually made a token gesture around Christmas, more for Thomas' sake than his parents. She would keep her coat on, the visit short, and radiated nothing like goodwill. Thomas was better at hiding his feelings, he had a lifetime of practice behind him. The drive gave him time to think, which sometimes was a good thing, sometimes not. It depended on his mood. Thomas was ruled by his moods, a legacy of his unstable childhood.

Growing up, he never thought his family was particularly different. He and his younger brother, Frank, got on well together. Frankie was a couple of years younger in age and a lifetime older in experience. He left as soon as he was old enough, never visited, never kept in touch, the strange filial duty that ruled Thomas lacking in his younger brother. A coldness that lay at the heart of Frank Senior was all too plain to see in Frank Junior. Thomas often debated with himself if he was weaker than his sibling but came to the conclusion that he just cared, something Frank Senior couldn't beat out of him. There were some happy memories from that era, they were just outweighed by the trauma of living with an abusive father. Frank Senior also had his moods, one thing at least that Thomas and his father shared.

It started out well enough. Old Frank started out as a happy-go-lucky sort of guy, a young family man starting out in the sixties, a time of opportunity and new beginnings. The problem was that when the seventies came around, Frank Senior was still in his dead-end, low paying job. Optimism died with the Beatles, opportunity never seemed to knock, at least not for Frank. Someone had to pay. Frank wasn't a drinking man, he despised those weak fools who escaped reality by the glass, and so concentrated all his efforts on the home front. In the beginning Frank cared. He cared too much. He didn't start out to be a bad father, and if asked today would say he never was, he just wanted to instil some discipline, give them direction, prepare them for what it was like out there. He wanted more from life, for himself, for them. Disappointment after disappointment, the constant struggle to make ends meet finally took their toll on his nerves, made him jumpy. A wife that seemed resigned to her lot and two kids who always wanted more was not the ideal sanctuary to return to after a forgetful day in the factory.

Frank arrived home on his clapped-out motorbike, noting the better cars sitting in his neighbours' driveways, the bigger and more expensive toys strewn about their gardens by cleaner and neater kids. Identical homes on each side of his somehow looked nicer, bigger even. Even their bloody grass was greener. He was usually in a foul mood even before he opened the hall door.

The boys were growing up fast. Thomas took after his mother, happy with his lot, eager to please, wanting to be liked. It drove Frank crazy. The younger son, Frankie, inherited more than just a name from his father. Even as a young child it took a lot to make Frankie cry. A hardness in the eyes, a steely look that promised payback, was unsettling to see in an eight year old. Thomas seemed to care more, and he paid for it. He was still paying for it.

He parked in the empty driveway of his parents' home, his father never got around to owning a car. As he approached the door it swung open and his mother stood there waiting for him, the insincere smile that she hid behind for the last thirty years pasted to her face.

'He's waiting for you, son,' she said, stepping aside to let him enter.

This was part of the usual routine. His mother never asked how he was, how was the journey, how was his life. A woman in denial. There was no outward show of affection, apart from the smile, and certainly no physical contact. Physical contact in this home usually denoted bruises and swellings, and the occasional trip to the emergency room, though to be fair to Frank Senior, that hadn't happened in many years. Age and time had mellowed him. Thomas made his way into the kitchen where his father sat at the table, his jacket on, the evening newspaper spread out before him.

'How are you Dad?' he asked brightly, trying to be upbeat.

'Can't complain, Son, can't complain,' said Frank Senior.

That's not how I remember it, thought Thomas, but said nothing. He took a seat opposite his father, his mother's smile upon his face. Frank Senior closed the paper carefully and folded it into his pocket. Only when he had read it from cover to cover would his wife be allowed to look at it. Not much had changed since Thomas' time. His mother took her seat on the sofa and resumed reading her novel, her romance came in page form these days. Thomas gazed out the window and admired the colourful flowers swaying gently in the fading light. His father was a keen gardener and the regimental lines and clean corners of his flower beds gave an insight into his frame of mind. Orderliness denoted control, and old Frank was still very much in control.

'The garden looks well,' Thomas said, just for something to say.

Frank nodded but didn't feel the need to reply, the garden always looked well.

'Shall we go then?' Frank said, getting out of his chair and jamming the newspaper firmly into his pocket.

Thomas rose quickly, car keys dangling in his hand.

'I'll see you, Mam,' he said to his mother.

She looked up expectantly, smile in place.

It occurred to Thomas, not for the first time, that he hardly knew his mother. He wondered if she was ever happy, ever regretted not running when she was still young enough to do it. Sometimes he felt she must have stayed for the sake of the kids yet he had few memories of a close bond between her and her children. Life back then was like walking on eggshells, tension and chaos just a heartbeat away. The reason for all that tension now passed Thomas, leading the way out to the car. Shading his father in both height and weight, Thomas wondered how this man struck terror into him and even now made him nervous and uneasy. He didn't have the answer.

The routine was always the same, Frank was a creature of habit and liked orderliness in his life. Thomas would drive the five kilometres to Frank's local bar, keeping a few points below the speed limit, for although Frank didn't own a car or even a licence, nevertheless he would comment if Thomas broke the speed limit. Rules were there for a reason.

The bar was only local in the sense that it was relatively close to the house. Although Frank had been going there every week for most of his adult life, none of the customers and only two of the barmen actually knew his name. He had no friends. They sat towards the back of the bar, away from the TV. Frank didn't enjoy TV if he couldn't change the channels when he wished. The back of the bar was quiet and ideal for long cosy chats, which made it even more awkward for both men as they usually had nothing to say. Long pregnant silences ensued, broken occasionally by Thomas humming to himself, a nervous disorder he had since childhood. Sometimes Frank resorted to his newspaper, completely ignoring his son. When this happened, Thomas sat and practised his mother's smile.

His father always bought the first round, two pints of Guinness, and waited patiently at the bar while they settled. Sometimes the barman would engage him in conversation and Frank was always polite, but something in his manner often caused the barman to walk away and serve someone else. Returning to the table, Frank placed the drinks carefully on the beer mats and took a seat next to his son. Over the years they had learned which subjects were safe to talk about, which ones were taboo.

Thomas always allowed his father to start things off, and some weeks they said nothing at all. Politics and religion were off limits as Frank held extreme views on both. He would ban religion, close churches and nationalise their assets. His politics were right wing. He would deport all immigrants, bring back National Service and the death penalty. There was no middle ground.

The only subject Thomas would have liked to talk about but never dared was his childhood, and why Frank saw the need to fight two young boys as if they were adults, man to man, no holds barred. It was something Thomas never spoke about although he once thought of going to a therapist. Maybe he could bring Frank along and get family rates.

In the end they usually spoke about gardening, a subject close to Frank's heart. His dream, which he told no one, was to retire to the warmer climes of the Mediterranean and cultivate a semi-tropical garden. Of course, on Frank's pension that was never going to happen, just another reason to p**s him off. So he spoke on the subject he felt comfortable with, and Thomas made all the right noises beside him.

Frank had never been to Thomas' home, he didn't 'do' visits, and would have been surprised to see both his front and back gardens covered in flagstones, not a plant in sight. Even Thomas didn't know if it was a subconscious way of getting back at his father but his wife seemed to like it and his own kids ran riot in the open spaces, which suited Thomas just fine.

Thomas went to the bar to get the drinks, a pint for his father, a half for himself, as he was driving. He returned to find his father reading the newspaper, which he continued to do until it was time to leave. Thomas sat and tried to hear the football scores coming in on the distant TV. He missed most of them. The drive home was in silence, though Frank seemed more relaxed after his couple of drinks. Thomas dropped him at the front door, but didn't go in.

'See you soon, Son,' Frank said, getting out of the car and making it sound like a threat.

'See you soon, Dad,' replied Thomas obediently.

The drive home was almost pleasant, the rush hour was over and traffic flowed freely. Thomas felt himself unwind as he got closer to his home, the ordeal with his father over for another two weeks. He drove into his driveway and was greeted by his own young son rushing out to meet him. His heart jumped for joy, he would never repeat the mistakes of the past. His four year old son jumped into his open arms and gave him a hug. Thomas felt happy for the first time that day.

'What would you like for tea tonight, Son?' he asked the mischievous boy.

'Can I eat my goldfish, Dad?' he replied innocently, serious eyes watching his father.

'How about some bread and jam instead?' asked Thomas, suppressing a smile.

'OK, Dad,' the child replied.

The goldfish could wait for another day. Father and son entered the house and closed the door, contented.

A BOX OF DREAMS
Hil Jennings

'. . . and there are reports from across the northern part of the country that many people witnessed something streaking across the night sky, perhaps some debris entering the Earth's atmosphere. But further to the south, on the outskirts of the town of Av-Al-Ahan, reports of a loud explosion in the early hours of the morning led to local police . . .'

'You look like something worn by an air hostess,' he jibed. 'Something on her lapel to give a sense of efficiency where none really exists.'

'Do you mind!' retorted the unicorn. 'I happen to be a very important mythical creature and I'll have you know I'm made of gold. Besides, they're called flight attendants now and I know a thing or two about flying.'

This was too much for the trader. He heaved his bulk from the low stool and, leaning towards the back of his curtained stall, swept the floating material aside as the hot breeze urged it to resist. He reached round into the relative darkness and felt for his weighing scales.

'Gold indeed!' he scoffed. 'We'll see about that!'

Squatting back down beside the dusty grass mat, the trader scooped up the unicorn brooch and, blowing it, he placed it carefully on one of the trays, raising the thumb ring just above the height of his forehead. With equal care, he placed one, two, and then a third coin on the opposite dish until they levelled.

'See,' the trader squinted as he joked, 'there are no scales before *my* eyes! I am Merkhim. And keep your legs still,' he ordered, 'it is not possible to cheat a professional, my friend.' Merkhim chortled triumphantly as the balance revealed its judgement. He held the unicorn in the palm of his hand. 'You are nothing but a brass trinket, proclaiming your inflated worth like so many others in the souk. But, for all your audacity, I like you. You will perhaps be useful to me after all.'

The unicorn sighed, desperately disappointed that after all the high hopes and expectations, she should find herself so scorned. She had failed to consider that her own status among the earthly creatures might be overstated and that the harsh environment of the market place might not be the ideal starting point for her own 'embodiment'.

Her journey into reality had been preceded by much research and she had eventually chosen to transform herself into a golden brooch after submitting a long and academic discourse entitled 'The Value and Place of Symbolism in Society'. Her intellectual discussions with a well-qualified leprechaun had also persuaded her that a post-graduate course in reality would be the way forward. Her studies had not been wide-ranging enough though, and reflecting on the arduous process of 'embodiment', she realised that there had been those in mythology who had cheated her, knowing full well she was unlikely to return. As she had lain on the scales, the true extent of the scam had begun to sink in.

She realised that at his command not to move her legs, she couldn't anyway. The fragile legs that had oddly remained flexible enough for her to walk this far were now also set hard, the force of the impact reversing the normal physical properties of cooling metal. Her spine was arched backwards, frozen in the posture of shock she had taken as the dragon had so callously torched her in order to send her here. She might even have described the look on the dragon's face as cold or unfeeling had it not been such a fiercely hot experience for her. It had not been the pleasant process she had imagined and now some of that heat was rising within her.

'This is not how it is supposed to be,' she wailed. 'I am supposed to be revered.'

'Why?' asked Merkhim. 'What purpose do you serve except to allow a dream to those who cannot face reality?'

'Dreams. Exactly! People must dream and I exist to serve those dreams. And now you hold me in the palm of your hand. I exist. I am the embodiment, the truth behind the dream. Behold, I speak do I not?'

'Rather too much, I think.' He clipped the brooch pin shut and grinned. 'You should have stayed where you were. Dreamers should learn that they ought to be thankful for what they have. Ambition and dreams . . . you have to be very careful!'

It was getting late and most of the town's inhabitants had made their purchases and returned to their houses for the evening meal. Merkhim tossed the unicorn into his shirt pocket and began to load his donkey with coloured silks and cottons, trays of necklaces and jewellery and his bag of tools. The unicorn lay upside down, pondering her circumstances as he rolled up the mat and tucked it in the last available space beside the beast's rump. He turned his face to the setting sun, sweeping the red check of his headscarf across the lower half of his wrinkled, oiled face. He greeted his fellow traders as they dispersed with a low 'Salaam, Allah protect you'. The dusty palm leaves at the roadside, silhouetted against a darkening landscape, seemed to bend down as though enquiring of Merkhim how well he had done at the souk. The unicorn, having now reasoned that her position was one of desperation, decided to try another tack.

'Merkhim,' she called sweetly, 'don't you ever have dreams? Things you long for? Things like wealth? You'd like more gold wouldn't you?'

'Do you hear that Ezza, my treasure?' Merkhim whispered into the donkey's ear. 'There are voices in the evening breeze. All the time they whisper to us but they do not know who we are. They know nothing about what our fathers taught us and they are not willing to learn anything either. These voices, my beauty, we must learn to recognise them for what they are; the voices of false dreams. If we had listened to such voices in the past, Merkhim would not be walking this road with such a faithful servant now.'

Apart from the sound of softly grinding footfalls there was silence for a moment as the unicorn expected a reply from the donkey. Then she remembered where she was and her frustration boiled over. The multiple indignities of being first deceived, then cast in metal and losing her status were hard enough to bear. Now she was being ignored in favour of a commonplace ass and treated like some . . . some object of derision! Fury streamed from her lips in a tirade of abuse.

'You filthy, disgusting, fat and ugly little man! How dare you treat me like this, you arrogant, vain, conceited, selfish prig. You are nothing but a mean, cheating liar who steals from all his customers and who smells like a heap of camel dung . . . or worse . . . you're a heap of steaming donkey droppings . . . and I hate you!'

The trader chuckled quietly and said nothing as the unicorn sobbed uncontrollably. They turned off the main thoroughfare, down a narrow track bordered by open concrete drains and low walls. Here were noises of children playing and radios blaring combined with the smells of both roasting and living goat. The unicorn became aware of the change and was silent. As they approached a pair of high steel gates, one was unbolted to allow them through.

'Grandfather, Grandfather!' A boy of about six smiled up at Merkhim. 'Is it finished yet?'

'Patience, Assad! It will be tomorrow or the day after. I think it is going to be even better than I promised,' he laughed.

'Even better?'

'Even better,' he reassured the boy, nodding.

'Can I unpack Ezza for you and give him some water?'

'Of course,' he crooned, 'I will just put my tools in the workshop and then we will eat. Too much talking has made Grandfather hungry today.'

As the boy set about his task, Merkhim tossed the tool bag on a workbench and felt in his pocket for the brooch. He reached for a pair of wire cutters and snapped the clasp from the back.

'What are you doing?' the unicorn asked in surprise.

'Just making sure you do not fly away, my precious, or should I say, my precocious one? I would not want to be parted from you now, would I? Sleep well.'

His words seemed to calm her. Perhaps she had misjudged him. His manner was certainly difficult to comprehend, but this was an entirely new world to her after all. Had he not said that she might be useful to him earlier on? Now he was saying he did not want to be parted from her. If she was to make the most of her circumstances, it seemed she ought to go along with him instead of antagonising him.

She lay as only she could lie. Nothing more than a brass brooch fashioned in the shape of a unicorn arching back and now with its pin cut off. *At least*, she thought, *I have my dreams.* She did as she was told and fell asleep to dream of the trader, of how he blew on her as though powerfully blowing her dross away. For all his fire, the dragon had not managed to do that. In fact, had he not put it upon her? She dreamed on, that his breath was his life story, a tale of his father losing great riches and of how Merkhim had found contentment making his living at the souk.

She never woke again. Two days later, Merkhim returned early from the souk with Ezza to find Assad eagerly opening the gate again, hardly able to contain his excitement. Merkhim, equally unable to contain his laughter, slapped his hand on the boy's back.

'Go on then my grandson! Ezza has something for you but you will have to find it!'

'Ezza, tell me, where is it?' Assad stroked the donkey's soft nose with his own but Ezza just nodded.

As he had done before so often, the boy carefully unpacked the bundles of material, the sacks of lentils and meal and the trays of jewellery. When at last he reached Ezza's striped blanket, he saw at once the protruding lump and reached underneath to pull out something wrapped in a dyed linen cloth. Slowly, he peeled back the material to let its tasselled edges dangle above his sandals and then he gasped as his eyes tightened. The glare of the late afternoon sun reflected into his face.

'Oh Grandfather! It's Ezza! It's Ezza! Look Ezza, it's you, see?'

Assad's mother came out into the courtyard.

'Look Mama! Look what Grandfather has made. It's my box but it's got Ezza on it, see?'

She took it from him and examined it. The carefully jointed corners of streaked brown olive wood were beautifully crafted and an intricately carved pattern interlaced around the base declared it to be a labour of love. The lid, however, was its crowning glory. The boy had expected a wooden box but not one so finely decorated with hammered and polished brass leaf. The edges were pinned in with the greatest accuracy and the outline of Ezza, punched into the surface so finely that it could have been engraved, bore the hallmark of a patient and steady hand.

'You spoil that boy,' smiled his mother.

'I wasn't expecting a brass lid. It's so shiny and beautiful!' continued the boy.

'Neither was I at first,' replied Merkhim. 'I'm glad you like it.'

'Like it? I've always dreamed about something like this! And with a donkey on it too!'

A PLACE IN THE SUN
Joyce Walker

'But you like Spain,' Maud said.

They were seated at the dining table in the small flat above Alf's Hardware Store. The shop his father had left to him when he died; the shop that had been his place of work since he'd left school, which was more years ago than he cared to remember.

His father had hoped that it would be a nest egg for them, something they could eventually leave to their own children, only he and Maud hadn't had any and now, with the big DIY store open in the precinct and taking all the trade and because of his advancing age, for the first time in his life he was thinking about retiring.

'Of course I like Spain,' he said. 'For two weeks of the year when I want a bit of sunshine, it's great, but to sell up and move? That's a different thing altogether.'

'So, you're just going to stay here and wait till there aren't any more customers because they can get everything cheaper round the corner, are you? What kind of man does that make you, Alfie Higgins?'

'A tired old man,' he said. 'That's what it makes me.'

'You're not old,' Maud replied. 'These days 60's no age at all. It's just that the climate in England is so depressing. A few weeks of Spanish sunshine and you'll be as good as new. Now eat your omelette and stop feeling sorry for yourself.'

For weeks now, Maud had been putting pressure on him to move abroad, but the fact of the matter was that he liked England and really had no desire to leave. As he picked up his fork it gave him no satisfaction at all to discover that even his omelette was a Spanish one.

She was right about one thing though, if he didn't sell up pretty soon, there wouldn't be a business left to sell, so after he'd finished breakfast he phoned the estate agent and put the shop onto the market.

Then he turned his mind to thoughts of what he wanted to do after the shop was sold. That put him in a real quandary, but one thing he was certain of, while it might involve moving to the coast, it certainly didn't feature moving to Spain, or anywhere else on mainland Europe for that matter.

Still, at every meal time, Maud would nag him relentlessly and he grudgingly agreed that some kind of compromise must be found, before she drove him totally insane.

'I've been thinking,' he said over a cup of tea in the small kitchen behind the shop where Maud, after her afternoon shopping trip, had decided to join him. 'If you're still keen to go and live in Spain, why don't you check things out and see what you can find.'

The look she gave him, the one that said, I knew you'd come round in the end, only served to harden his resolve to do some checking of his own.

Days passed and the pile of glossy brochures with homes to buy on the Costa grew. Every evening Maud would thrust another one under his nose and tell him how ideally situated it was. As if that wasn't infuriating enough, she had also taken to walking round the house singing, 'Viva Espania', and saying 'Óla', instead of 'hello'.

The next step in his plan was to get her out of the way for a while, so he suggested she took her sister with her to look at some of the houses to see if any of them were suitable. He, of course, would have to stay at home so he could show round prospective buyers.

What he didn't tell her was that he'd already accepted an offer and it was a much better one than he'd expected, enough to buy the villa in Spain and also for another venture he had in mind, one that wouldn't mean flying, or sailing, to foreign shores.

So, while Maud was looking for her dream home, Alf packed a case, got in the car and headed for Southwest.

The guest house was perfect. Close enough to the sea to be able to advertise it with a sea view and the revenue it would generate in the summer, provided he and Maud budgeted well, would enable them to escape during the winter months to that place in the sun Maud dreamed about.

The best of both worlds and he'd tell her so when she came home.

'I've found the perfect place to live.' The words spoken almost in unison.

'All we have to do is sign the papers and hand over some cash.'

Maud looked at Alf in disbelief. 'You can't have found the perfect place to live,' she said. 'I'm the one who's been looking.'

'Ah,' he said, 'actually, we've both been looking, only in different parts of Europe, and I've devised a plan that will keep us both happy, though for the next few years it will mean a bit of hard work.' Then he said, 'How would you rate your breakfasts, cooked breakfasts that is, on a scale of one to ten?'

Maud had always been good when it came to full English. 'About eleven, why?'

'Me? I'd give it at least twenty, and your housekeeping skills are second to none.'

'I'm pleased you think so,' she said, 'but where's all this flattery leading? I've a feeling I'm not going to like what you're going to say next, so spit it out so I can throw something at you.'

'There's this place in Newquay, needs no work at all and already has a regular stream of visitors through the summer months. They don't expect much, just a clean room with a TV and a kettle which are already installed and good food. Bed and breakfast only, of course.

'Bed and breakfast? You want me to run a B&B? You're older than I thought. I think your mind's finally gone.'

'Hear me out. We've got a buyer for the shop, a very generous one as it happens. Only for the shop, which means we can let this flat out to a tenant. Everybody wants flats round here, and for the right rent it wouldn't take us long to find one. The money from the shop will buy your villa in Spain and pay a good slice of the money for the B&B.'

'What's the point of having a villa in Spain if we're not going to live there?' Maud asked, rather sullenly.

'We rent it out to holidaymakers in the summer, so we're getting revenue from that, and then, when the weather turns inclement, and the holiday trade has finished in Newquay, we take ourselves off to the sunshine for the winter. Your dream and mine combined.'

'What happens when we get too old to keep your dream going?' she asked.

'Then we'll have a clearer idea about whether we want to continue to live your dream, or whether to sell up and cruise round the world for a few years. Come on, Maudie, you know it makes sense.'

She knew it did, but wished it didn't. After a long silence that Alf thought was never going to end, she replied, 'Si Senor, but I'll want to see this B&B of yours before I finally commit myself.'

'You'll love it,' he said confidently. 'They have palm trees in Newquay, you know.'

'Yes and they have vineyards in Spain. Let's celebrate with a glass or two of Sangria.'

THE SCHOOL REUNION
Wendy McLean

Lucy went into the hall to pick up the bundle of morning post laying on the mat, she bent down to pick it up. 'Goodness, a lot of mail today, all bills I suppose,' she mumbled to herself. She went back into the living room and sat at the dining room table, as she started to go through it she noticed a card. 'What's this?'

Lucy began to read it. You are invited to attend a school reunion at the Rugby Club on June 18th at 7.30pm. RSVP Jean Smith by the 2nd August. *Oh it would have to be her doing it, she always did like organising big events,* thought Lucy, she'd have to think about this one.

Suddenly she felt a hand placed on her shoulder. 'What's that Mum?' said her young son interested.

'Oh nothing, it's only an invitation.'

'Let's have a look.' Before she could stop him it was snatched out of her hand.

'Thomas! Really! That's awfully rude, give it back to me!'

'Why don't you go, see all your old friends, you haven't been out for ages since Dad died.'

'We'll see,' she said.

It had been hard for her to cope since losing John, she'd thought they would grow old together, retire and buy a nice cottage by the coast, oh how wrong she had been.

Lucy got up and walked into the kitchen, her cup of tea and toast still left on the worktop, a tear suddenly rolled down her cheek, the very mention of John always seemed to reduce her to tears, she must become stronger for her children's sake.

Lucy took her handkerchief from her dressing gown pocket and wiped the tears from her eyes and then walked back into the living room. She glanced down at the card left on the table where Thomas had left it. Again the words came into her mind. *I can't possibly go*, she thought.

Half of them would be old and fat with high up jobs etc, bragging about how well they'd done, since leaving school and then being asked by one of them in a sarcastic way, 'And what do you do?' No she couldn't possibly go. It was only two weeks away and whatever would she wear. *No, I can't go*, she repeated it over and over in her head.

'You have to go Mum,' the voice startled her.

'Not you as well Katie!' she said.

'It would be good for you Mum.' Lucy looked at her daughter, she had long red hair, slim figure, *just like I was at seventeen, pity her dad wasn't here, he would have been proud of her.*

Katie had done well at college gaining GCSE A and B grades, very different from her old mum, never clever at school, but then times were different for my generation.

In her moment of daydream the phone began ringing. 'I'll get it Mum,' said Katie.

Lucy waited and listened. 'Hello 519247. Who should I say is calling?'

'Jean Smith.'

'Just one moment please, I'll get her for you.' Katie then reappeared.

'Mum, it's Jean Smith, wants to know if you're going to the school reunion?'

'Right!' replied Lucy.

'Go on Mum,' said Katie hurrying her mother into the hall.

Lucy picked the receiver up. 'Hello Jean,' she said.

'Will you be coming to the reunion? It'll be awfully good fun,' said a loud voice at the other end, *did she have to put on such a posh voice* thought Lucy, the boys at school had a nickname for her 'Horse Box' because she always thought everybody fancied her especially when they saw her in her riding horse gear.

The conversation continued. 'There's quite a lot going, I've even managed to get a few of the old teachers. You remember old 'Jones', all the girls fancied him, we all thought he looked like Richard Burton, probably old and fat, still good for a laugh. Ha ha!'

Did she have to laugh like that, Lucy could just picture Jean in one of those old St Trinian's films.

Lucy suddenly burst out laughing and promptly replied, 'Yes all right, I'll come.'

She replied, 'Splendid, see you soon.'

'Bye!' said the voice at the other end.

Lucy put the phone down and made her way back into the living room, 'You're going then Mum?' asked Katie.

'Yes I suppose I am.'

The week before the reunion, Lucy decided to take herself, Katie and Thomas out for a day in Leicester. They all had an amusing time going in and out of the shops, although after a while poor Thomas became bored, complaining he needed food urgently for his stomach.

'Can't we go and eat? This is boring women's stuff!' moaned Thomas.

After a while a decision was made to go and eat, much to the delight of Thomas. 'Yes! McDonald's here we come! Food!'

And so they made their way to McDonald's. Thomas rushing through the entrance door and before we could stop him, up to the counter he went blurting out, 'I'll have a double cheeseburger and fries.'

'Wait a minute young man,' said Katie, 'we haven't ordered ours yet!'

With this Thomas marched off in a huff and sat down at one of the tables and placed his hands to his head in frustration.

After lunch Katie decided she wanted to look in one of the book shops, much to Thomas's annoyance who constantly repeated, 'I want to go home, I'm tired,' he moaned.

He soon got his request later and as we made our journey home in the car Thomas worn out by his day lay fast asleep on the back seat.

On the evening of the reunion Lucy was getting increasingly nervous, she looked at the pale blue outfit laid on the bed, a casual dress and jacket, nothing over the top and in any case it wouldn't be worn again for some time, she never went out much anyway.

Quickly she dressed and stood in front of the long bedroom mirror, admiring the way she looked. *Um! Not bad for a woman of fifty,* she thought. As she stood there she almost thought she saw an image of her husband by her side reflected in the mirror.

'You look lovely,' the voice suddenly sounded so real.

'John!' she whispered softly, her hand reaching out to touch the glass, but there was nothing there.

Lucy sat down on the bed in a daze, she felt the emotion swell up inside her but no tears came, composing herself Lucy made her way downstairs.

Thomas and Katie sat watching the TV. 'I'm going now,' she said.

Lucy made her way to the front door, they hadn't even noticed how nice she looked, typical.

As she was halfway through the door two voices suddenly shouted, 'You look lovely Mum!'

A broad smile came across Lucy's face as she walked towards her car, they had noticed after all.

It was ten miles to the Rugby Club at Welland and Lucy arrived in good time, she drove into the car park and found a space quite easily. Getting out of the car she walked towards the entrance, she felt very nervous. *Right here goes*, pushing the door open she was met by laughter and noise of the crowded room, cigarette smoke filling it like a blanket of fog. Lucy found herself searching the room for familiar faces and then a voice from behind startled her. 'Hello Lucy old girl.' Slowly she turned around.

Lucy stared at the man in front of her, the face wrinkled with age, he wore a brown tweed jacket and baggy cord trousers. 'Bob Coles, well how lovely to see you. Still got your farm at Bulwick?' said Lucy.

'Struggled in the last few years with this er foot and mouth, right bugger it's been, nearly lost it.' Bob Coles had never married although he'd always had a bit of a soft spot for her at school. His mother had died young, but his older sister had brought him up so his father could carry on working the farm.

Bob Coles' face beamed with a huge smile, he spoke suddenly, looking straight at Lucy, 'Mmm, I always said Lucy Edwards, you'd bring a good price at the market, you're still a fine looking woman.'

As they stood talking some other school mates joined them and as the evening went on Lucy was pleased she'd decided to come.

Bob Coles stayed with her most of the evening, telling her about his farm and how in a few years time he wanted to retire up to Shap Wells in Yorkshire and buy a small cottage. Lucy envied him in a way, he'd worked hard all his life on the farm, and she suddenly asked him why he'd never married.

'Well it's never really bothered me, never met the right one woman I suppose,' he said.

'Did you marry?'

'Yes, I've got two children, a boy, Thomas and Katie my daughter,' she suddenly opened her bag and produced a small photograph and gave it to Bob.

His eyes glanced over it, 'Lovely children, you and your husband must be very proud of them,' he said.

Lucy suddenly became very quiet as her eyes started to fill with tears.

'What's the matter?' said Bob, 'Have I said something wrong?' he asked, concerned.

'No, it's not you, I lost my husband three years ago, he became ill quite suddenly.'

'I'm so sorry,' said Bob.

Lucy then found herself telling him everything, how it had been such a shock when the doctors had found the tumours in John's head and how after a few months he was gone. 'Do you know Bob, if it hadn't been for the children I don't think I could have coped.'

Talking to Bob had really made her feel much better, suddenly Bob came out with a suggestion. 'Why don't you and the kids come down and see the farm one weekend, we could have some lunch down my local pub if you want to, of course no pressure or anything you understand.'

Lucy was quite surprised by this and took some time to answer, 'I couldn't possibly give you an answer without asking the kids first, you do understand don't you?' she said.

Lucy looked at Bob, he had a kind face, deep-set forehead, blue eyes, thick dark eyebrows. He looked rather like Sigbried out of the popular veterinary series on television, he even talked a bit like him. Lucy really liked him, he hadn't changed since school, she felt really sorry to disappoint him but perhaps there was another way. But before she could say anymore he got up and walked away leaving Lucy very disheartened.

As the evening went on Lucy met many of her old friends, most of them talking about the old days at school, families etc and the evening turned out a success.

But Lucy never got the chance to talk to Bob again and explain until Jean Smith said to her, 'You were well in with Bob Coles, anything to report, do tell me. You know I like a bit of gossip darling, I bet he's got loads of money, he is a bachelor after all.'

Lucy decided to tell Jean what Bob had suggested and how foolish she felt at turning his offer down. 'Leave it with me,' she said, 'I know Bob quite well, I'll talk to him and see if he'll ring you, it's worth a try,' said Jean.

'That's really good of you, thanks Jean,' replied Lucy.

'Only too pleased to help, after all if it makes you happy,' she replied.

The evening came to a close and everybody said their goodbyes and went. As Lucy arrived home she noticed the lights were still on in the house. It must be Katie waiting up and wanting to know how she got on. She got out of the car and made her way to the front door but before she had even placed the key in the door it opened and there stood Katie. 'Well, had a good evening?' she asked.

'Not now, I'll tell you all about it tomorrow,' and with this she made her way up the stairs to bed, closing the door she burst into tears. *Oh why didn't I take up his offer, what a foolish woman you are.*

Next day Katie and Thomas wanted to know all, Lucy began to tell him about Bob Coles and how he'd invited them all down to stay one weekend at his farm and how very disappointed he'd been at her refusal. They both sat listening until Thomas suddenly said, 'I've never been on a farm. I could take my bike and ride it round the country lanes.'

'Oh Mum, why didn't you say yes?' Katie nodded in agreement so it was two against one.

'Perhaps he'll telephone, we'll wait and see,' said Lucy giving both her children a big hug.

She got up from the chair she was sitting on, suddenly the phone began ringing, Lucy hurried to the telephone, she picked the receiver up. 'Hello Lucy, it's Bob Coles, Jean asked me to give you a ring,' he said. 'Have you thought anymore about my offer?'

'Yes I have Bob. The children and I would love to come,' she replied.

'That's great, next weekend be all right? I could pick you all up if you like,' he said.

'That would be lovely and thanks again Bob, you're so kind,' said Lucy.

'Bye, see you soon.' And with that the call was finished much to the delight of her two children who stood listening in the doorway.

So the reunion hadn't been a bad idea after all, perhaps this was the start of a new beginning, Lucy smiled for she knew that John would have approved.

DANIEL KELLY
Margaret Pawson

1918

The steam train pulled into the station, spewing its cargo of war weary, khaki clad servicemen, onto the crowded platform. Daniel Kelly jumped out of the overcrowded carriage and edged his way through the throng of wheelchairs and walking wounded, his eyes searching the cheering crowd of excited women and children; some of which waved union jacks, others responding with outstretched arms to shouts of recognition but his beloved Mary was nowhere to be seen.

He stared at them sadly for a moment as he nestled amongst the maimed and blind, waiting for their loved ones to reach them but no one came forward for Danny, no one even spoke to him. Sometime later, as he watched the crowd melt away, with long lost sweethearts walking hand in hand, he knew a sense of disappointment, he also knew that Mary wasn't coming.

He looked into the snow laden sky, noting that however bad it looked, it was at least free of Zeppelins, then ambled alone down the snow covered, cobbled main street which would eventually lead him home. It had been eight months since he had been home, when, before embarkation, he and his neighbour, Joe Dowling had shared a forty-eight hour leave together. Danny shuddered at his memories, for in a barrage of shellfire, Joe had joined the ten million fallen, just two days before the armistice had been signed.

The snow was falling steadily as he reached the cottage, where on his arrival, he found Joe's widow, Bernadette attending Mary in childbirth.

Upstairs, Bernadette piled more logs onto the small fire, over which boiled a large pan of water. She looked at the small clock on the mantelpiece, which told her that it was 2am and never before had a night seemed so long. The faded curtains billowed in the draught from the cracked window making Bernie shiver, for although the fire was ablaze it afforded little heat. She pulled the curtains aside and looked through the glass, only to find her vision barred by the high bank of frozen snow, halfway up the window.

If the doctor doesn't get here soon, he'll not get through, she thought uneasily. In the big brass bed, Mary tossed and groaned; her face was pinched and drawn, her eyes deep set and fearful, while her white knuckled hands clutched at the hand sewn patchwork quilt with each excruciating spasm. Though the room was cold, her hair was entangled with sweat which ran in rivulets down her face and neck.

Bernie was worried, for Mary was small and it was well known that first babies were never easy, what's more it seemed to be lying wrong somehow and the child was struggling to be born.

'Ber-nie, oh Ber-nie!' she screamed.

Outside the wind howled mercilessly. In the silk draped, four poster bed, Dr Smith snuggled closer to his wife, cocooning himself against her soft, warm body as they lay in the hollow of the feather mattress. Oh he hoped he wouldn't be disturbed tonight for he was exhausted. Most of his patients were falling like flies, with the 'Spanish flu', most of which were proving fatal.

It was 12.30am when the call came. Reluctantly he pulled himself out of bed and throwing his clothes on over his night-shirt, ran quietly down the red carpeted stairs, along the oak panelled hallway and out into the white blanketed street, then set out on foot. By the time he reached the bridleway, he was exhausted but undeterred, he hunched his shoulders against the cold and battled on, hoping he would reach Mary in time.

Much later, he stopped for a moment to catch his breath and looked around at the once familiar patchwork of fields which had quickly transformed into an Arctic landscape. He couldn't see a wall anywhere and knew with a sense of panic, that he had lost all sense of direction.

He lifted his lantern higher but could see nothing except driving snow, swirling in front of him but he pressed on, struggling through drifts waist high, until sometime later he came upon a half buried signpost. It was then he realised that he had been walking in the wrong direction. He knew he had been a fool to even attempt it and told himself that he had better keep moving, for if he rested he could find himself buried in a snowdrift. He took a sip from his hip flask, congratulating himself on his foresight to bring it, as he felt the warm, comforting vapours hit his throat and chest.

Breathing more easily now, he made his way towards the copse, the only visible landmark on the bleak horizon. He knew that it would at least afford him a modicum of shelter.

Quietly, Bernie opened the bedroom door and carrying the lamp high in front of her, made her way down the cold, stone steps to the kitchen. Daniel did not speak on her arrival, for on entering the room, the sight of her stilled his tongue. He stared at her through the lamplight, willing her to move but she did not stir, only the muscles of her worried face twitched, as she stared into the embers of the dying fire. He sat close to her clasping her hands but she failed to notice. Instead, she began to pray, 'Oh, help me Father, help me get this night over, then I will cope, I have got to cope . . .'

He put his arm around her shoulder for they both needed reassurance but she did not respond. How long she sat in this way, Daniel could not say for a call from upstairs alerted them both.

'Ber-nie, Bern-ie!'

Rubbing her tear ridden face on the corner of her apron, she hurriedly made her way upstairs, followed more slowly by Danny, as though he knew already what lay ahead. From the doorway he looked at his wife. Her face was as white as death as she tossed her head from side to side on the pillow.

'Dan-ny, Dan-ny, where are you?' she called in a hoarse whisper, and he knew she was letting go of life.

'Hang on lass, hang on, Doctor won't be long.'

Once inside the copse, Doctor Smith paused for breath. His throat felt rough and his body was being attacked with a raging heat. He sat exhausted on the bole of a tree, where he gulped what little there remained in his flask but this time it did little to soothe him, it only succeeded in making him hotter. He found himself muttering as his body shook with fatigue and sickness.

Sometime passed before he staggered his way out of the copse. As he skirted the woodland the force of the blizzard bent his body double but he struggled against it. Even his footprints had disappeared under a fresh blanket of snow but from his vantage point he could make out the dim outline of the church spire in the valley below. It was all he needed. It would lead him home, home to his bed.

'Sorry Mary,' he muttered feverishly to himself, 'I tried but failed miserably.'

It was towards morning when Mary gave out an ear piercing scream, as with her last ounce of strength she pushed her baby into the world. As the child drew its first breath, Mary drew her last.

Daniel fell onto his knees, burying his head in Mary's limp body and lost his reason.

Bernie stared lovingly at the motherless child, a beautiful girl child. Her tiny head which topped the heartshape face, was covered with downy blonde hair, and the childless Bernie knew that she would love her. Tenderly, she wrapped her in a shawl and placed her in the washbasket by the fireside while she prepared Mary for her last journey.

Danny, lifted his head from the cold surface of the highly polished table. He opened his aching eyes, which throbbed with the pulsations attacking his brain but they were only able to take in part of what was happening. In desperation he reached for his bottle and finding it empty, sent it crashing into the hearth, wafting ash from the dead embers and scattering the fire irons against the fender. He stood, swaying a little, for sorrow, heavy and deep, born of desperation and loneliness pulled at him. Terrorised with the knowledge of what had happened, he staggered back, clutching the armchair, where he sat spread-eagled and motionless.

It was two days before anyone reached the cottage. A knock on the door stilled the silence. Wearily, Bernie dragged her tired body to the door and was surprised when standing before her was, not the doctor but Father Durkin.

Even when the priest entered the kitchen, Danny did not move, only his black rimmed eyes lifted towards the ceiling where Mary lay in their bedroom. His face took on a sadness, a resignation.

On seeing the priest, Bernie sobbed pitifully, clutching the child to her empty breast as she rocked to and fro in her sorrow. Father Durkin sighed, for the anxiety and grief which had come upon this household could not fail to make itself felt by those who entered it. 'Come Bernie, don't take on so, you must find strength for this child needs you.'

And so continued his words of comfort, until time had stretched for a full hour, when pulling his purple stole from his neck and folding it reverently in his battered case, he turned to her saying, 'Pray for strength Bernie, pray, remember, out of the depths . . .'

Daniel stared with eyes blinded with despair, at the dim outline of the priest, who stood before him obscuring the light from the solitary candle.

'O, why do we listen to you, Father. Get yourself away, go on, get out,' he roared but the priest just sighed, touched Bernie's shoulder and left quietly.

Danny reached for the bottle, for once filled with whiskey, he would forget, his grief would be dulled and nothing would penetrate his befuddled state.

Mary Kelly took her last ride on the flat cart. Daniel stood dry eyed, waiting behind the makeshift hearse with his head bowed, then walked aimlessly behind the priest as the funeral cortege made its way down the snow packed track.

'In nomini patris, et filii, et spiritus sancti . . .'

The monotonous tones of the priest echoed in his eardrums, reverberating through his body, like the aftermath of an exploding shell. His mind was once again back in Galipoli. He saw himself running across an open space, amid the blast of artillery fire. He saw an exploding shell throwing him in the air, bringing him down to earth amid a pile of limbless, dying comrades. He saw himself crawling, the while dragging Joe Kelly, trying to reach the dug out. Blood ran in his eyes, blinding him but even though he could not see, he knew that Joe was dead.

'I am the resurrection and the life . . .'

They had arrived. The churchyard was bleak and silent, except for the raucous screeching of some hungry crows in the treetops. His heart felt as cold as the weather but his body radiated warmth as it was overcome with a strange pressure which urged him forward to the graveside.

'Dust thou art . . .' chanted the priest.

Daniel lifted his bowed head, his eyes coming to rest on the black marble tombstone,

Mary Kelly
Wife of the late Daniel
Killed in action
9.11.18

The pressure in his body threatened to overwhelm him as realisation hit him. He was dead then. He closed his eyes and saw it all clearly; he was in Galipoli, he saw the barrage of gunfire intensify, he felt the force of the explosion, lifting him as another shell burst before him.

'Amen,' the priest ended.

On the headstone sat a young woman, her long flaxen hair blew in soft tendrils in the icy wind.

'Look, Bernie, look it's Mary,' he whispered but Bernie neither saw nor heard him. He closed his eyes and gave in to the force overpowering him and joined his beloved Mary. Then, hand in hand, they walked together into eternity.

LAST LOOK ROUND
Sarah Sproston

I didn't want to open my eyes. I could feel the sun creeping in through the cracks in the curtains. Mocking me. I turned the other way and pulled the covers over my head. Would it matter if they forgot about me and left me to rot in this place that I would always consider my home? Taking me from the only place I could feel peace. I'd grown up right here, why should I leave? This is where I belong, how can they think it's right to take that from me? They knew this was killing me, but pretending not to notice . . .

'Come on sweetheart, you know you should be up by now. We've all got a lot to do,' my mother spoke soothingly, predicting my foul mood, as she peeled back the covers from my face. 'Breakfast is on the table.'

She only needed one second of my hard stare for her to flee my room.

I counted every step, as if it were my last, down the stairs. I stopped before I reached the bottom, my toes feeling the carpet between them. I could hear the chatter in the next room, just like a normal morning. Except it wasn't a normal morning; it was our last. I closed my eyes as a tear slipped down my face, remembering the uncountable times I'd gone storming up these same stairs, floods of tears, to my only sanctuary. I took the final steps and turned the door handle. Silence. Everyone's faces turned to me, expecting some typical explosion of emotions. I wouldn't give them the satisfaction. I pushed the door closed behind me as the sound echoed through the empty house. I sat down, not looking anyone in the face, feeling their gazes on me. The conversation slowly resumed. Inside I was laughing. They thought their precaution was saving me. I sat there, silently, listening to that mindless chatter, no one dared to mention a word about what was happening that day. I finally looked at each of them in turn. My mother, a glint of hope in her eyes that today would end it all; the 'new start' would make things better. She had no idea. My father, a drink in his hand, the hard stare at Mother, the reluctance to accept any of this as real. My brother and sister, talking happily between themselves, the innocence of youth shining in their smiles.

I'd had enough. I pushed away from the table, away from the perfect family, and fled to my room. I heard Father get up, planning to stop me from ruining our last day as a family, but Mother stopped him. I don't know how. Guilt overwhelmed me; I couldn't imagine what he did to her for standing up to him. A smashed glass; a muted scream; a slammed door. I could picture the same old scene: Mother kneeling on the floor, holding a shaking hand over the throbbing, swelling welt somewhere on her body; telling her two children everything was OK. They would ignore the situation. The chatter would stop, but the concerned looks were quickly hidden. They didn't understand; how could they?

Not even I understood. How could a father, a husband, plague his loved ones with such a fierce temper? He'd poisoned the whole family, and now he was tearing us apart.

I crawled into the corner of my room, shaking with fear; fear that the next scream would be mine. I pulled my knees up to my chest, holding myself, comforting myself, knowing that this love would never come from one of those monsters. I was losing it, I couldn't take it. I was completely alone, the way I liked it; yet all I ever longed for was for one simple hug, one simple sign that someone cared.

'I don't need any of you!' I screamed over and over, my voice breaking with this climax of emotion, this inner conflict that would never cease. I collapsed to the floor, waiting desperately for someone to come to see that I wasn't OK. No one came. Alone; only because I had no other choice.

By midday the 'incident' at breakfast had been cleared away, and, on the surface, completely forgotten. Why bother to argue? They presumed that day would be the last; we would be gone and so would he. But he would never be gone; the bruises faded, the cuts healed, the wounds could be tended to, but the scars? No, they would haunt us forever.

The empty rooms, the packed up boxes, the silence lingering in every corner; I was ready to explode. Running away from things seemed to be my speciality; but there was one person I had to say goodbye to. The one family member I ran to, and not from.

Those streets; streets I should have played on, fallen over and grazed my knees on; those streets were glad to see the back of my family. Tears smeared my make-up, black rivers bleeding down my face as I struggled to put one foot in front of the other. My whole world was in pieces.

I knelt at her grave; the wind blew my hair across my tear-streamed face. I did not attempt to pull it back; I didn't want her to see me cry, I didn't want her to know why. I longed to stay there, to stay on my knees and be with her for eternity. How could I say goodbye to the only person I knew loved me?

As I dragged myself to my feet and turned away, I tried to, God help me I tried, but the word choked in my throat, and I told her I'd see her soon.

Returning to 'my home' I was sick with anger. No one had noticed I was gone. Silently I climbed the mountain for the very last time. My room was bare, naked; there was no trace of me ever existing. I sat in the centre of this box that had once been the only place I could be me. Now where was I to be me?

The door creaked open; I didn't have to turn to know it was him.

'We're almost ready,' he paused, taking a breath. 'You can be happy. It won't haunt you anymore. I won't be there. Things will be better . . .' Another breath. 'I'm sorry.'

I turned and he was gone. The door was closed. I stood and looked out of my window. Father got in his car, one last look up, and drove away.

The sun that had scorned at me that very morning now looked down on me, smiling. That was goodbye. Maybe that was the end, maybe he wouldn't come looking for us, and maybe I was finally free. The removal van was full; the house was empty. It was time for me to say goodbye.

As the car reversed off the drive, I felt nothing. That looming shadow had not departed; it would follow me for the rest of my life. I watched the house, my home, disappear. My heart sank. I pulled my hood over my head, and once again I made the sun fade away.

TICK TOCK
Lorraine Middler

'Tick tock, tick, tock, when will the clock stop?'

Susan sat listening to the solitary sound of the clock as she had done so many times before. Only this time it was different. At last she was free, about to start a new life. An hour from now she would be out of this life which held such terrible memories.

At 21, she had never had a social life, never had a boyfriend, never experienced anything other girls her age did on a regular basis. Her day consisted of getting up at 5am, tidying the house, preparing breakfast for Mum and Dad and washing up before starting her job at the post office at 7.30am. She had to come home at lunchtime to prepare her parents' lunch and then back to work until 4.30pm. Then the same scenario - home to prepare dinner, tidy up, do the washing and ironing and run baths for her parents. Eventually, she would fall into bed around 11pm, totally exhausted.

Susan's colleagues at the post office were under the impression that her parents were disabled, admiring her for taking such good care of them and she did not disillusion them. The truth of the matter was that her parents were cruel, selfish and as able-bodied as she was. They had treated her as a slave for as long as she could remember.

'Tick, tock, tick, tock, when will the clock stop?'

She remembered vividly the darkness of the cupboard under the stairs, which she came to know better than any room in the house. She also recalled the fear coursing through her body if she was five minutes late coming home from school. Her father bellowed, 'You little brat, under the stairs, now!' She would hear the bolt being pulled across and knew she would be there for hours, sometimes all night. Always the same sound, 'Tick, tock, tick, tock!'

The cupboard still filled her with fear. She didn't have to visit it quite as often these days or the chores would not have been done but every so often her father would come home in a drunken rage. He would drag her out of bed forcefully, utter obscenities, tell her what a worthless waste of space she was and throw her in the cupboard.

The next morning she would wake to her father roaring, 'Where is that useless girl? I want my breakfast!' The events of the previous night would then dawn on him and he would drag her from the cupboard and yell, 'Get my breakfast, quick smart, or else!' She was constantly bruised and aching all over from the mistreatment and in recent years from sheer exhaustion at being worked so hard.

'Tick, tock, tick, tock, when will the clock stop?'

Twenty minutes and she would be gone - free!

Time to make sure everything was organised prior to her departure. Her suitcases were all packed in the hallway and last night's dinner dishes were all washed, dried and put away. In fact the house was like a new pin. She re-read her letter to Aunt Pearl, then popped it back in the envelope. She did not seal it as she would have to put her keys inside after she'd locked up.

She heard the taxi's horn as she lifted the clock off the wall in the hallway and smashed it to the floor.

As she picked up her cases and passed the stair cupboard she laughed evilly, 'No more tick, tocks - at long last the clock has stopped!'

Susan left the house, locked the door, slipped her door key into the envelope containing the letter to her aunt and sealed it.

A big smile filled her face as she got into the taxi. 'Airport please, Sir and could you stop at a post box en-route?' She lay back on the seat, proud of herself, like the cat who'd got the cream.

It had all been so easy really, she recalled smugly. She had the full trust of her boss and he had allowed her to lock up and put everything away in the safe many times before. However, this being a holiday weekend, there was more than normal in the safe on Saturday. Enough to last Susan a long, long time, she gloated. When she went home that night she was brighter than usual, although a bit apprehensive. She prepared dinner as usual but didn't eat herself, stating she had too much work to do.

As usual her parents had eaten hungrily and fallen asleep within half an hour afterwards. The sleeping pills had worked quickly. She had then gagged and bound them, dragged them to the cupboard under the stairs and bolted it firmly. That night Susan had the soundest sleep she'd had in years. She heard scraping noises coming from their temporary home but had no problems ignoring it. Aunt Pearl would find them in a few days and Susan would be long gone.

She knew there would be complete silence in their temporary prison - not even the reassuring 'Tick tocks' - as the clock had well and truly stopped. As for Susan, however, the clock was just starting as her new life began!

VELVET ANGEL
Rupert Young & Daisy Chelton

I found some photographs in my late mother's house. A face saddens me. This girl - a ballerina type, American, golden hair, legs of air - got entangled with punk culture then gangsters, who got her homeless with alcohol and drugs. She died in a yachting accident.

'Amelia Fischer, Amelia Fischer, Amelia Fischer! You get in first!' hollers a voice full of adventure; the photos are taken on the river near Arundel.

Skipper Jacobs checks the gold hands of his wristwatch, motionless for a second.

'Let go forward, cast off!'

Daisy and Amelia Fischer draw his attention to any promising inlets in the farthest bank, perching in the bow of the steadily advancing dinghy; one was the hidden entrance to a wild-fowling decoy.

By and by, the way was established for penetration - along a reedy fleet - into the decoy's world of forgotten stillness, festooned with water lilies, unpuzzled by tides, unmentioned by guides and clearly signposted, *Danger! Tree feeling hazard!*

With oars creaking the boats cut through a carpet of dazzling ripples: the two girls at the bow, Katie on her seat in the sternsheets, Skipper Jacobs rowing carefully, to avoid something.

We were ashore at a staithe where the alder opened out:

'Hey, Daisy! There's a swinging tyre over some water! You could swing on it! There's a pull rope!'

'What's a pull rope?'

'Hey, I wish we could go swimming! Could you swim in here?' asks someone.

'You haven't got any things, maybe you could find somewhere shallow to paddle instead?' says the man with a beard, and to Amelia, ' . . . Okay 'Velvet'?'

Amelia Fischer waits for this man to wander further off, then she rolls her eyes to Heaven. I suppose she would be about sixteen.

'You could paddle over here,' says Daisy as she begins to demonstrate a way down to the water's edge. Then she slips.

'Daisy! Watch out!' Amelia tried to snatch her arm. 'Daisy!' but Daisy went.

Splash! Her face crumples, water in her shoe. She crouched down, hanging onto the bank with both hands.

'Don't look, don't look!' she bursts.

Amelia looked, Daisy was spread-eagled. She was on dry ground, but her sock was all wet.

'Do you want to make it up to that garden place then and see the others?' Amelia was saying to her, carefully. She hoped Daisy wouldn't burst into tears here.

'I've got mud on my leg!'

'And it's all over the back of your plimsoll,' offered Amelia without knowing why she did. (It meant so little to her . . . 'Amelia Fischer' never meant mud or crumpled-down socks or caught with her jersey (or cardie) rucked up - like she's been caught out - which is why this photo looked different). Daisy twisted, standing on one leg to catch her other foot. When she saw it she freaked out.

Skipper Jacobs approached. He was fat and he was oldish - nice though. 'Aah dear, that's dunni-daint it 'Angel'?'

Amelia Fischer went with Skipper Jacobs, pulling her short skirt over her legs as she sat neatly down under a tree. Where they lay the earth sloped to an evil-smelling pond, through sun spurge. Later, he was hugging her.

There was no way to reach across to the swinging tyre. That swinging tyre was impossible to swing on. Daisy could see that, we all could.

Daisy lost her sense of adventure and wanted to go.

'Let's take a photograph!' someone volunteered to the other man. 'All of us, here under the cherry blossom!'

Skipper Jacobs and that new, dishevelled Amelia Fischer, gratefully holding Daisy's hand, and the other orphans at the decoy, all grouped together for the 'velvet' man to catch them in the sunshine all those years ago.

WHO'S UP THERE?
Marc Shemmans

'Bob,' Pauline whispered in the darkness, 'Bob?'

Bob groaned and turned over to face her. 'Huh?'

'Did you hear that noise?'

She knew he hadn't; he'd been sound asleep and snoring.

'Hear that noise?'

'There was a noise in the attic.'

Bob groaned once again. 'What sound? What . . . sort of . . . sound?'

Covered by the duvet all the way up to her neck, she glanced up to the ceiling, even though Bob wasn't even looking at her.

'It sounded like banging.'

'Mmm, it's probably just mice or rats.' He shrugged, and sighed.

'Bob!'

'What?'

'You know very well it wasn't mice or rats!'

'How do I? I didn't even hear it!'

'So what shall we do?'

'Go back to sleep, I'm sure it's nothing.' He rolled onto his side, turning his back on Pauline. As he adjusted his pillow, the sound came again. He flopped onto his back. Though Pauline couldn't see his face in the gloom, she knew he was looking at the ceiling.

'Did you hear it that time?' she asked.

He nodded.

'We've got to do something.'

'Oh come on, it's got to be rats!'

'Are you serious?'

'It's got to be.'

'That's bulls**t. You know it isn't rats!'

'What do *you* suggest we do then?'

'Go up there.'

'You?'

'You must be joking,' she scoffed, '*you* can go up there.'

Another sound came. This time it was the noise of a floorboard creaking above the bedroom as if someone had taken a very careful step. Not wanting to be heard.

'Maybe you'd better just call the police.' Pauline whispered to him.

'No,' Bob told her abruptly, 'if it isn't rodents then it's probably just the house settling.'

'Be serious Bob.'

'Look Pauline, nobody's up there.'

'How do you know?'

'It's an old house. Old houses have rats and mice and can make funny noises.'

'Not that funny.'

'Just ignore it.'

'We can't ignore it!' she said incredulously.

'You know it's unsafe up there, that's why I've had to lock it up so no one will go up there and get hurt.'

'You'll just have to be careful then.'

Bob rolled onto his side to face her. 'For the last time there is no one in the attic.'

'I'm going to call the police.' Pauline pulled the duvet off of her and began to climb out of the bed.

Bob grabbed her arm too tightly and let out a sigh of exasperation. 'Very well, I'll go and have a look.'

'Do you have some sort of weapon?' she asked him. 'A baseball bat or something?'

'Don't worry; I won't need anything because nobody is up there. All I need is a mouse trap.'

'Terrific,' Pauline muttered.

At the bedroom door, he flipped on the light and then turned to her, 'I'll be back soon.'

She heard his quick footsteps out on the landing and heard him switch the light on. Then she listened to the distinct sound of her husband unbolting the door to the attic and making his way up there.

After a few moments she heard another sound from above. This time it was much louder - it sounded like two people scuffling. She closed her eyes and tried not to think about it, but then she heard a heavy thud that sounded like someone falling to the floor. It sent chills racing down her spine and she just sat there on the bed and continued to listen.

Five minutes later there was total silence.

Ten minutes later she was shaking in fear but somehow she managed to force herself out of the bed. She padded softly over to the attic door which was slightly ajar.

I don't want to go up there. But where is Bob?

She stood at the door for several moments, silently listening. There were no sounds, so she grabbed the door knob and pulled the door open.

'Bob?' she called into the darkness of the attic. 'Is everything okay?'

'I'm okay.' Bob called down to her and a torrent of relief swept through her entire body.

She switched on the light which was at the bottom of the attic stairs and began to ascend when Bob called down to her. 'Stay there!'

'Are you okay?'

'Yes.' He couldn't conceal the anxiousness in his voice.

'Are you sure?' she asked.

She flinched and paused, but then a moment later she began to creep up the stairs. She felt a strange swelling in her throat, a wild scream about to break free. And then she heard the groan on the staircase above her. She glanced up and saw Bob. Only this wasn't the Bob she knew. This wasn't the man she had been married to for ten years. This man was an insane monster.

He was lumbering down the stairs naked. His body was scarlet with dripping blood and in his right hand he held a butcher's knife, in his left was the decapitated head of a woman.

This had to be a joke, Pauline thought. But somehow she knew that it wasn't.

Screaming, she lurched backward and shouted at him, 'Bob! What are you doing?'

'I told you to go down Pauline and you didn't listen, you had to be an interfering b***h!'

'What on earth are you talking about?'

He held the woman's head up before him. 'She had been up in the attic for days Pauline. I had been having my fun with her, like I had with all the others before her. But this one got a little noisy so I've had to end her life even earlier. Usually I keep them for a week before I dispose of them Pauline, but because of *you* she had to go early.'

Pauline turned and began to run but something struck her in the back and an instant later, she fell onto the floor of the landing.

She tried to force herself up, and that was when she felt Bob slide the knife out of her back. She felt his hands. Enormous hands, that had caressed her lovingly many times before, but these hands were now uncaring and slippery with blood and would do even worse things to her, things that even in her worst nightmares she wouldn't have imagined could happen.

For a moment she knew that none of this was happening - none of this could happen - because this sort of thing didn't happen in real life. But it was happening and it was happening to her.

Bob picked her up, flung her over his shoulder, and carried her up the attic stairs and dropped her onto the dusty attic floor - right next to the headless corpse of the woman. He fastened her hands and feet with a thick blood-soaked rope. Now she knew why her husband always locked the attic, it wasn't because it was unsafe up here, it was because this was his abattoir, the place where he kept his darkest, sickest secrets from her and now she had become one of those dark, sick secrets.

She screamed but Bob ignored it and pointed the knife at her. 'Now it's time for some fun.'

He laughed, and that laugh seemed like the worst sound she'd ever heard in her life.

CALL MY BLUFF
Eric Dawson

It was a late autumn cold afternoon. I was sat staring into a log fire oblivious of my wife and her daughter being present. I am expecting two visitors but not on a social call, my solicitor and a barrister. The latter I am hoping can get me off a rape charge which I am completely innocent of, and at the present all I can see is a prison sentence for something I haven't done. That sounds like the doorbell and they are here. I answer the call and go to the door, inside they are introducing themselves to my wife and her daughter. Then it's down to business.

'Now Mr Davis . . .'

'Please call me Peter.'

'Right Peter, I don't have to tell you how serious this charge brought against you is. So will you tell me exactly what happened that afternoon in July. And for now I am Tony.'

'Right, this is the truth. It was a hot, sunny afternoon, my wife June and her daughter had a day out in the city shopping. I decided to put something on casual and sit by the swimming pool and all I had on were my shorts sitting in a sunbed chair, I then heard a car coming down the drive, I knew who it was and knew she was in for a surprise as the wife was shopping. She got out of her car and said hi. It was then I told her that June was shopping. She replied, 'Oh silly me, I forgot, she told me she wouldn't be here.' She then asked if it would be alright if she had a dip in the pool, which I replied, 'It's there, use it!' Then oddly she asked if she could get ready in a spare bedroom. 'If that's what you want but the dressing room and the shower is OK, here.' But she said she would rather go upstairs which she did. She hadn't been in the bedroom long before she called out of the open window.

'Peter, can you come up, I want you.' I thought *what's gone wrong*, and went up to see her and when I got there I could see what her game was, she was standing in her bra, panties and suspender belt. 'What do you want?'

Her answer, 'Isn't it obvious.' 'May hay while June is away, I will give you a good time.' I wasn't pleased and told her so. I told her 'I don't know what your game is but don't expect me to play it. I suggest you get dressed and leave this estate faster than you come on it and don't make another visit to it.' And I went back to my sun lounger. It wasn't long before she came down to her car and called me a pig and said I will be sorry, and no one refuses her of sex. And she left, and that is truth Tony.'

'And I believe you Peter, how long have you known her?'

'Not all that long, I have only been married to June 12 months and she was one of June's best friends and attended the wedding. Then the next time I saw her was when June made arrangements for a foursome with her husband to go for a meal, I remember the night well. When we came back for drinks someone had attempted to force the lock on the door, her husband said, 'Once bitten twice shy, get yourself a good security system put in, I can recommend a good firm!'

'But you never did Peter?' asks his barrister.

'No.'

'Right Peter, I have come up with a good idea. Let me tell you what I think we should do.'

After telling Peter of the idea, asks him, 'What do you think of that?'

'I will go along with that 100%,' says Peter.

'Right, well come Thursday, the trial, we will keep our fingers crossed.'

The trial

Thursday morning 10am the court is ready for the trial. The judge appears and all stand. How the trial begins. Peter is asked to take the witness box.

Then the judge asks him, 'Your name please?'

'Peter Davis Sir.'

'Mr Davis you are brought before this court with the serious charges of rape on the 11th of July how do you plead?'

'Not guilty Sir.'

'You may leave the witness box. Prosecuting councillor, call your first witness.'

And he calls for Mrs Ruth Skinner.

'Could I have your name please?'

'Mrs Ruth Skinner.'

'Mrs Skinner, would you tell the jury what happened on the 11th of July.'

'I went to my friend's home, Mrs June Davis on a hot sunny day for a chat and a swim. On arriving there I was told that June was out all day shopping, then I remembered she did tell me she was going shopping. Well, seeing as I was there, I asked Mr Davis if it would be alright if I had a swim to cool down. 'Sure he said, but you will have to go upstairs to get undressed, the dressing room and shower are not working here on the patio.' So I went upstairs in a spare room and I had got half my clothes off and all I had on was my bra and knickers. When in the room came Mr Davis. I was so shocked I said, 'Do you mind Peter, what do you want?' His answer was, 'You know what we both want, you knew June wasn't here so let's not pretend.' I said, 'Peter, June is my best friend and I wouldn't even think about doing a think like that on her.' Then he grabbed me and forced me on the bed, I was screaming and crying and pleading not to rape me but it was all in vain, he was too strong for me, I called him a pig, and he said he was sorry. I got dressed as soon as I could to get home and report him to the police which I did. The police arrived and when I told them what had taken place they had a doctor to examine my bruises.'

'Thank you Mrs Skinner, no more questions.'

'The defence offers no questions at this stage.'

'The prosecution councillor asks for Dr Dobson to take the witness box.'

'Dr Dobson when you were called to see Mrs Skinner what did you find?'

'I found that she was rather distressed. Bruises on her thighs and breast as though she had been through a struggle.'

'Your witness,' pointing to the defence, but the defence doesn't want to question the doctor.

The defence councillor asks for Mrs Skinner to take the witness box please.

'Now Mrs Skinner, under oath you have told the jury what happened on that day. I ask you as Mr Davis' defence, if he is found guilty what would you like as his punishment?'

'I would like him to get life in prison and rot there.'

'That's plain enough of your feelings for Mr Davis, and with what the jury have heard I think they would find him guilty. On what they have heard, Mrs Skinner did you go to Mrs Davis' wedding?'

'Yes.'

'And about a month after the wedding did you and your husband go for a meal with Mr and Mrs Davis?'

'I believe so.'

'Yes or no Mrs Skinner?'

'Yes.'

'And after the meal it was suggested that you all went to Mr Davis' home for drinks, is that so?'

'Yes we did.'

'When you got to the house what then?'

'Well we went in for drinks.'

'But there was something before you went in Mrs Skinner, what was that?'

'Sorry I don't know.'

'Let me refresh your memory, was there something wrong with the door? Someone had attempted to break in.'

'Is that right Mrs Skinner?'

'Yes, I remember, that's right.'

'What did your husband say? Let me tell you what he said. 'Once bitten twice shy Peter, get yourself a good protection system, with your valuables and the size of this house you want CCTV in every room and I know just the firm to do it.' Is that right Mrs Skinner?'

'Yes, he did suggest that.'

'Now you are beginning to tell the truth, for what you have said in the past is nothing like the truth, you are a vindictive and impulsive liar to suit your evil and vicious jealous means. Do you know what this is Mrs Skinner?' he said holding a video tape in his hand.

'It looks like a video tape to me.'

'That's right, that's what it is, and that there is a TV and video recorder which I requested be in the court room. Now, remember what your husband said, get yourself a good CCTV system in all your rooms. Now Mrs Skinner, I give you two options. One you can tell this court the truth or I put this tape in the recorder and it isn't pleasant viewing, take my word for that, but if you insist you were raped than I show the jury what's on this tape. So Mrs Skinner, did Mr Davis rape you on the 11th of July?'

Mrs Skinner breaks down in tears.

Now the judge has his word.

'Mrs Skinner, you must answer the question. Did Mr Davis rape you, yes or no?'

In a soft voice she answered, 'No.'

'Mrs Skinner we cannot hear you, can we have that clear, loud voice we had at the beginning of the trial?'

'No, no he didn't rape me.'

'Mrs Skinner, are you aware of what you have done in this court of law? Under oath in that witness box you have held this court in contempt, and for that you will face this court at a later date and facing a custodial sentence. Mr Davis on the evidence I have just heard there are no charges against you and you are free to leave this court. You the jury, thanks for your service and you are free to leave this court. Could I see both councillors in my chambers please.'

In the judge's chambers all three meet and the prosecuting councillor is the first to congratulate Tony the defending councillor.

'But Tony, I am mystified.'

'So am I,' says the judge.

'Well let me try and solve your mystery, what is it,' asks Tony.

'Well, on the charge against him I could understand having a barrister of your standing, but when you produced that tape as evidence what did he want you for? If as you say what you have on the tape he could have avoided this trial by showing the police on the very first day he was charged, so do I take it you lied in court Tony, when you said what is on the tape doesn't make pleasant viewing?'

'At no time did I lie, at no time did I say he had CCTV in the rooms, I did say what's on the tape doesn't make pleasant viewing.'

'So what's on the tape, Tony?' asks the judge.

'The cruelty against the Jews in the concentration camp and that doesn't make pleasant viewing. I played a game, it's called *'Call my bluff'!*

INFORMATION

We hope you have enjoyed reading this book - and that you will continue to enjoy it in the coming years.

If you are interested in becoming a New Fiction author then drop us a line, or give us a call, and we'll send you a free information pack.

Alternatively if you would like to order further copies of this book or any of our other titles, then please give us a call or log onto our website at www.forwardpress.co.uk

New Fiction Information
Remus House
Coltsfoot Drive
Peterborough
PE2 9JX
(01733) 898101